PUFFIN BOOKS

COMET IN MOOMINLAND

Books by Tove Jansson

COMET IN MOOMINLAND

FINN FAMILY MOOMINTROLL

THE EXPLOITS OF MOOMINPAPPA

MOOMINSUMMER MADNESS

MOOMINLAND MIDWINTER

TALES FROM MOOMINVALLEY

MOOMINPAPPA AT SEA

MOOMINVALLEY IN NOVEMBER

Tove Jansson

COMET IN MOOMINLAND

Translated by Elizabeth Portch

PUFFIN

PUFFIN BOOKS

Published by the Penguin Group
Penguin Books Ltd, 80 Strand, London WC2R ORL, England
Penguin Group (USA) Inc., 375 Hudson Street, New York, New York 10014, USA
Penguin Group (Canada), 90 Eglinton Avenue East, Suite 700, Toronto, Ontario, Canada M4P 2Y3
(a division of Pearson Penguin Canada Inc.)
Penguin Ireland, 25 St Stephen's Green, Dublin 2, Ireland
(a division of Penguin Books Ltd)
Penguin Group (Australia), 707 Collins Street, Melbourne, Victoria 3008, Australia
(a division of Pearson Australia Group Pty Ltd)
Penguin Books India Pvt Ltd, 11 Community Centre, Panchsheel Park, New Delhi – 110 017, India
Penguin Group (NZ), 67 Apollo Drive, Rosedale, Auckland 0632, New Zealand
(a division of Pearson New Zealand Ltd)
Penguin Books (South Africa) (Pty) Ltd, Block D, Rosebank Office Park, 181 Jan Smuts Avenue,
Parktown North, Gauteng 2193, South Africa

Penguin Books Ltd, Registered Offices: 80 Strand, London WC2R ORL, England

puffinbooks.com

First published in Finland as *Kometjakten* 1946
This translation published in England by Ernest Benn Ltd 1951
Published in Puffin Books 1967
This edition published 2012

002

Set in Plantin
Printed in Great Britain by Clays Ltd, St Ives plc

British Library Cataloguing in Publication Data
A CIP catalogue record for this book is available from the British Library

ISBN: 978-0-141-34528-4

www.greenpenguin.co.uk

CONTENTS

CHAPTER 1   7

Which is about Moomintroll and Sniff following a mysterious path to the sea, pearl-fishing, the discovery of a cave and how the Muskrat avoided catching a cold.

CHAPTER 2   27

Which is about stars with tails.

CHAPTER 3   37

Which is about how to manage crocodiles.

CHAPTER 4   42

Which is about the meeting with Snufkin and a terrible experience with a giant lizard.

CHAPTER 5   52

Which is about the underground river and rescue by a Hemulen.

CHAPTER 6   63

Which is about the adventure with the Eagle and the finding of the Observatory.

CHAPTER 7   77

Which is about how Moomintroll rescues the Snork Maiden from a poisonous bush and in which the comet appears in the sky.

CHAPTER 8   92

    Which is about the Village Stores and a party in the forest.

CHAPTER 9   108

    Which is about a fantastic crossing of the dried-up sea and how the Snork Maiden rescues Moomintroll from a giant octopus.

CHAPTER 10   125

    Which is about a Hemulen's stamp-collection, a swarm of grass-hoppers and a horrible tornado.

CHAPTER 11   137

    Which is about a coffee-party, the flight to the cave and the arrival of the comet.

CHAPTER 12   156

    Which is about the end of the story.

CHAPTER I

Which is about Moomintroll and Sniff following a mysterious path to the sea, pearl-fishing, the discovery of a cave and how the Muskrat avoided catching a cold.

THE Moomin family had been living for some weeks in the valley where they had found their house* after the dreadful flood (which is another story). It was a wonderful valley, full of happy little animals and flowering trees, and there was a clear narrow river that came down from the mountain, looped round Moominhouse and disappeared in the direction of another valley, where no doubt other little animals wondered where it came from.

One morning – it was the morning that Moomintroll's pappa finished building a bridge over the river – the little animal, Sniff, made a discovery. (There were still plenty of things left for them to discover in the valley.) He was wandering in the forest when he suddenly noticed a path he had never seen before winding mysteriously into the green

* It was painted blue. Moominhouses usually are. *Translator.*

shadows. Sniff was spellbound and stood gazing at it for several minutes.

'It's funny about paths and rivers,' he mused. 'You see them go by, and suddenly you feel upset and want to be somewhere else – wherever the path or the river is going perhaps. I shall have to tell Moomintroll about this, and we can explore it together, because it would be a bit risky for me to go alone.' Then he carved a secret sign on a tree-trunk with his pen-knife, so that he could find the place again, and thought proudly: 'Moomintroll *will* be surprised.' And after that he scooted home as fast as he could so as not to be late for lunch.

Moomintroll was just putting up a swing when Sniff got home. He seemed very interested in the mysterious path, and directly after lunch they set off to have a look at it.

Half-way up the hill on their way grew a clump of blue-trees covered with big yellow pears, and of course they couldn't get past that without Sniff deciding that he was hungry.

'We'd better only take the windfalls,' said Moomintroll, 'because mamma makes jam from these.' But they had to shake the tree a little so that there *were* some windfalls.

Sniff was very pleased with their haul. 'You can carry the provisions,' he said, 'because you haven't got anything else to do, have you? I'm too busy to think about things like that when I'm the Path Pioneer.'

When they reached the top of the hill they turned and looked down at the valley. Moominhouse was just a blue dot, and the river a narrow ribbon of green: the swing they couldn't see at all. 'We've never been such a long way from home before,' said Moomintroll, and a little goose-fleshy thrill of excitement came over them at the thought.

Sniff started to snuffle about. He looked at the sun, felt

the direction of the wind, sniffed the air, and in fact
behaved in every way like a great Path Pioneer.

'It should be somewhere here,' he said busily. 'I made a
secret sign with my knife on a plum tree just where it
began.'

'Could it possibly be here?' asked
Moomintroll pointing to a curly flourish on a tree-trunk on the left.

'No! Here it is!' screamed Sniff,
who had found another curly flourish
on a tree-trunk on the right.

At the same time they both caught
sight of a third curly flourish on a tree-
trunk right in front of them, but it
was terribly high up, at least three
feet above the ground.

'That's it, I'm sure,' said Sniff
stretching himself. 'I must be taller
than I thought!'

'Well, strike me pink!' exclaimed
Moomintroll looking around. 'There
are curly flourishes everywhere! And
some of them are nearly a hundred
feet up. I think you've found a haunted
path, Sniff, and now the spooks are

trying to stop us using it. What do you say to *that*?'

Sniff didn't say anything, but he got very pale about the nose. And at that moment a cackle of spooky laughter broke the silence, and down fell a big blue plum, which nearly hit Moomintroll in the eye. Sniff gave a screech of terror and ran for cover, but Moomintroll was just angry, and had decided to have a look for the enemy when, all of a sudden, he saw who it was. For the first time in his life he was face to face with a silk-monkey!

She was crouching in the fork of a tree: a small, dark, velvety ball. Her face was round and much lighter than the rest of her (about the colour of Sniff's nose when he had washed rather carelessly), and her laugh was ten times bigger than herself.

'Stop that horrible cackling!' shouted Moomintroll when he saw that she was smaller than he. 'This is *our* valley. You can go and laugh somewhere else.'

'Wretched wretch!' muttered Sniff, pretending he hadn't been frightened. But the silk-monkey just hung by her tail and laughed louder than ever. Then she threw some more plums at them and disappeared into the forest with a parting hoot of evil laughter.

'She's running away!' screamed Sniff. 'Come on – let's follow her.' So off they rushed, scrambling headlong through bushes and brambles under a perfect rain of ripe berries and fircones, while all the little animals underfoot escaped into their holes as quickly as they possibly could.

The silk-monkey swung from tree to tree in front of them; she hadn't enjoyed herself so much for weeks.

'Don't you think it's ridiculous (puff) to run after a silly little monkey like that,' panted Sniff at last. 'I don't see (puff) that she matters.'

Moomintroll agreed to this and they sat down under a tree and pretended to be thinking about something important. The silk-monkey made herself comfortable in the fork of a tree above them and tried to look important too; she was having nearly as much fun as before.

'Take no notice of her,' whispered Moomintroll. Out loud he said: 'Good spot this, isn't it Sniff?'

'Yes. Interesting-looking path too,' Sniff answered.

'Path,' repeated Moomintroll thoughtfully. And then he suddenly noticed where they were. 'Why, *this* must be the Mysterious Path,' he gasped.

It certainly looked most mysterious. Overhead the branches of the plum-trees, oaks and silver poplars met and formed a dark tunnel which led away into the unknown.

'Now we must take this seriously,' said Sniff, remembering that he was the Path Pioneer. 'I'll look for by-paths, and you knock three times if you see anything dangerous.'

'What shall I knock on?' asked Moomintroll.

'Whatever you like,' said Sniff. 'Only don't talk. And what have you done with the provisions? I suppose you've lost them. Oh, dear! Do I have to do everything myself?'

Moomintroll wrinkled his forehead dejectedly but did not answer.

So they wandered farther into the green tunnel, Sniff looking for by-paths, Moomintroll looking for dangerous intruders, and the silk-monkey leaping overhead from branch to branch.

The path wound in and out of the trees getting narrower and narrower, until at last it petered out altogether. Moomintroll looked baffled. 'Well, that seems to be that,' he said. 'It ought to have led to something very special.'

They stood still and looked at each other in disappointment. But as they stood a whiff of salt wind blew in their faces and a faint sighing could be heard in the distance.

'It must be the sea!' exclaimed Moomintroll with a whoop of joy, and he started running upwind, his heart thumping with excitement, for if there is anything Moomintrolls really love it is bathing.

'Wait!' screamed Sniff. 'Don't leave me behind!'

But Moomintroll didn't stop till he came to the sea, and there he sat down and solemnly watched the waves rolling in, one after another, each with its crest of white foam.

After a while Sniff came out from the fringe of the wood and joined him. 'It's cold here,' he said. 'By-the-way, do you remember when we sailed with the Hattifatteners in that dreadful storm, and I was so sea-sick?'

'That's quite another story,' said Moomintroll. 'Now I'm going to bathe.' And he ran straight out into the breakers, without stopping to undress (because of course Moomintrolls don't wear clothes, except sometimes in bed).

The silk-monkey had climbed down from her tree and was sitting on the sandy beach watching them. 'What *are* you doing?' she cried. 'Don't you know it's wet and cold?'

'We've managed to impress her at last!' said Sniff.

'Yes. I say, Sniff, can you dive with your eyes open?' asked Moomintroll.

'No!' said Sniff, 'and I don't intend to try – you never know what you'll see down there on the bottom. If you do it don't blame *me* if something awful happens!'

'Pooh!' said Moomintroll diving into a big wave and swimming down through green bubbles of light. He went deeper and came upon forests of crinkly seaweed swaying

13

gently in the current – seaweed that was decorated with beautiful white and pink shells – and even farther down the green twilight deepened until he could see only a black hole that seemed to have no bottom.

Moomintroll turned round and shot up to the surface where a big wave carried him right back to the beach. There sat Sniff and the silk-monkey screaming for help at the tops of their voices.

'We thought you were drowned,' said Sniff, 'or that a shark had eaten you up!'

'Pooh!' said Moomintroll again. 'I'm used to the sea. While I was down there I got an idea – a good idea too. But I'm wondering if an outsider should hear it or not.' And he looked pointedly at the silk-monkey.

'Go away!' Sniff said to her. 'This is private.'

'Oh, please tell!' entreated the silk-monkey, for she was the most inquisitive creature in the world. 'I swear I won't breathe a word.'

'Shall we make her swear?' asked Moomintroll.

'Well, why not?' answered Sniff. 'But it'll have to be a proper swear.'

'Repeat after me,' said Moomintroll, '"may the ground swallow me up, may old hags rattle my dry bones, and may I

never more eat ice cream if I don't guard this secret with my life." Go on now.'

The silk-monkey repeated the swear, but she was a bit careless over it because she could never keep a thing in her head for long. 'Good!' said Moomintroll. 'Now I'll tell you. I'm going to go pearl-fishing and then I shall bury all my pearls in a box here on the beach.'

'But where shall we find a box?' asked Sniff.

'I shall hand that job over to you and the silk-monkey,' replied Moomintroll.

'Why do I always have to do the difficult things?' asked Sniff gloomily. 'You have all the fun.'

'You were the Path Pioneer just now,' said Moomintroll. 'And besides you can't dive. So don't be silly.'

Sniff and the silk-monkey set off along the beach. 'Wretched wretch!' muttered Sniff. 'He could have looked for his own old box.'

They poked around for a bit, but after a time the silk-monkey forgot what they were supposed to be doing and began to hunt for crabs instead. There was one that always careered off with his odd sideways gait and hid himself under a stone, so that they could only see his eyes, which were out on sticks and waved threateningly at them. They followed him for a long time until he jumped into a crack in the rock and built a wall of sand round himself so that they couldn't get at him.

'Well, he's gone anyway,' said the silk-monkey. 'Come on! Let's climb the rocks!'

It was a wild bit of coast, the rocks steep and jagged. After they had been climbing for a bit they found themselves on a narrow ledge above the sea, with a sheer rock wall on one side, and a steep drop to the sea on the other.

'Are you too frightened to go any farther?' asked the

silk-monkey, who found all this very easy, having four legs herself.

'I'm never afraid,' answered Sniff. 'But I think the view is better from here.'

The silk-monkey grinned jeeringly, and pranced off with her tail in the air. After a time Sniff heard her laugh. 'Hallo!' she shouted. 'I've found a house for myself – not a bad house either!'

Sniff hesitated a moment, but he couldn't resist the thought of the house. (He had always loved houses in unusual places.) So he shut his eyes tightly and set off along the ledge. The spray drenched him several times, and he offered up a prayer to the-Protector-of-all-Small-Beasts. Never in his life had he been so frightened or felt so brave as he did creeping along that ledge. Suddenly, he tripped over the silk-monkey's tail and opened his eyes. She was lying on her tummy with her head stuck into a hole in the rock, talking and laughing nineteen to the dozen.

'Well?' said Sniff, 'where's this house you were talking about?'

'In here!' screeched the silk-monkey, and she disappeared completely into the rock. Then Sniff saw that it was a cave, a real cave, such as he had always dreamed of finding. Its mouth was rather small, but inside it opened out into a big room. The rocky walls rose smoothly up to a gap in the roof which let in the sunlight, and the floor was covered with smooth white sand.

The silk-monkey scuttled off to a cranny in one corner of the cave and started to sniff and poke at the sand.

'There may be a lot of crabs here,' she cried. 'Come and help me look!'

'Don't disturb me,' said Sniff solemnly. 'This is the biggest moment of my life so far, and it's my first cave.' He smoothed the sand with his tail and sighed. 'I shall live here for ever,' he thought. 'I shall put up little shelves and dig a sleeping-hole in the sand, and have a lamp burning in the evenings. And perhaps I'll make a rope-ladder so that I can go up to the roof and look at the sea. Moomintroll *will* be surprised.'

And then he suddenly remembered Moomintroll's pearl-fishing and the box. 'I say, silk-monkey,' he said, 'what about that box? Do you think Moomintroll really needs it?'

'What box?' asked the silk-monkey, whose memory was exceedingly short. 'Come on! I think it's beginning to get boring here.' And in a twinkling she was out of the cave, back along the ledge, and down on the sand again.

Sniff followed slowly. Several times he turned round and looked back at the cave proudly. He was so full of it that he quite forgot to be afraid on the dangerous ledge, and he was still deep in thought as he trudged along the beach to the place where they had left Moomintroll, pearl-fishing.

There was already a row of shining pearls, and out in the breakers Moomintroll was bobbing up and down like a cork, while the silk-monkey sat on the sand busily scratching herself.

'I am the treasurer,' she said importantly. 'Now I've counted these pearls five times, and each time it comes to a different answer. Isn't that extraordinary?'

Moomintroll waded out of the water with his arms full of oysters; he even had several on his tail. 'Phew!' he said, shaking the sea-weed out of his eyes. 'That'll do for today. Where's that box?'

'There weren't so very many good boxes on this beach,' said Sniff. 'But I've made a great discovery.'

'What was that?' asked Moomintroll, for a discovery (next to Mysterious Paths, Bathing and Secrets) was what he liked most of all. Sniff paused and then said dramatically:

'A cave!'

'A real cave?' asked Moomintroll, 'with a hole to creep in through, *and* rocky walls, *and* a sandy floor?'

'Everything!' answered Sniff proudly. 'A real cave that I found myself.' He winked at the silk-monkey, but she was counting the pearls for the eighth time, and wasn't bothering herself about the cave any more.

'That's splendid!' said Moomintroll. 'Wonderful news. A cave is much better than a box. We'll take the pearls there at once.'

'That's just what I had thought of doing myself,' said Sniff.

So they carried the pearls to the cave and arranged them neatly on the floor, and then lay down on their backs looking up at the sky through the gap in the roof.

'Do you know something?' said Moomintroll. 'If you fly hundreds and hundreds of miles up into the sky you come to where it isn't blue any more. It's quite black. In the day time too.'

'Why's that?' asked Sniff.

'It just is,' answered Moomintroll. 'And up there in the dark are great sky-monsters, such as scorpions, bears and rams.'

'Are they dangerous?' asked Sniff.

'Not to us,' replied Moomintroll. 'They only snap up a few stars now and again.'

Sniff pondered this deeply and after a while they stopped talking and just lay watching the sunlight, which poured through the roof, creep over the sand and shine on Moomin-troll's pearls.

It was late in the evening when Moomintroll and Sniff got back to the blue house in the valley. The river flowed with hardly a ripple under the bridge, which showed up

vividly in its new coat of paint, and Moominmamma was arranging shells round the flower-beds.

'We've had supper,' she said. 'You'd better see what you can find in the larder, my dears.'

Moomintroll was hopping with excitement. 'We've been at least a hundred miles from here!' he said. 'We followed a Mysterious Path, and I found something terribly valuable that begins with P and ends with L, but I can't tell you what it is because I'm bound by a swear.'

'And I found something that begins with C and ends with E!' squeaked Sniff. 'And somewhere in the middle there's an A and a V – but I won't say any more.'

'Well!' said Moominmamma. 'Fancy that! Two big discoveries in one day! Now run and get your supper, dears. The soup is keeping hot on the stove. And don't clatter about too much because pappa is writing.'

And she went on laying out shells, one blue, two white and a red, in turns, and it looked very fine indeed. She whistled quietly to herself and thought there was rain in the air. A wind was getting up, and now and again a strong gust shook the trees turning their leaves inside out, and Moominmamma noticed an army of clouds massing on the horizon and beginning to march up the sky. 'I do hope there isn't going to be another flood,' she thought, picking up some shells that were left over, and going into the house as the first drops of rain began to fall.

In the kitchen she found Moomintroll and Sniff curled up together in a corner, tired out by their adventures. She spread a blanket over them and sat down by the window to darn Moominpappa's socks.

The rain was pattering on the roof, and rustling outside, while far away it dripped into Sniff's cave. And deep in the forest the silk-monkey crept farther down into her hollow tree and folded her tail round her neck to keep warm.

Late that night when everybody had gone to bed Moominpappa heard a plaintive noise. He sat up and listened. The rain gushed down the drain-pipes, and somewhere a shutter banged in the wind. Then came the pitiful sound again. He put on his dressing-gown and went to have a look round the house.

He looked into the sky-blue room, into the sun-yellow
one and into the spotted one, and everywhere it was silent.
At last he drew the heavy bolt of the door and looked out in
the rain. His torch lit up a strip of the path and raindrops
glittered like diamonds in the light.

'What in the world have we here?' exclaimed Moominpappa, for on the steps sat something wet and miserable,
with shiny black eyes.

'I am the Muskrat,' said the wretched creature faintly.
'A philosopher, you know. I should just like to point
out that your bridge-building activities have completely
ruined my house in the river bank, and although ultimately

it doesn't matter *what* happens, I must say even a philosopher does not care for being soaked to the skin.'

'I am most extremely sorry,' said Moominpappa. 'I had no idea that you lived under the bridge. Please do come in. I'm sure my wife can make a bed up for you.'

'I'm not a great one for beds,' said the Muskrat, 'they are unnecessary furniture really. It was only a hole I lived in, but I was happy there. Of course it's all the same to a philosopher whether he is happy or not, but it was a good hole . . .' After these words, which were not intended to be ungracious, he managed to gather enough energy and enthusiasm to go into the house, where he shook the water off him and said: 'What an extraordinary house this is!'

'It's a Moominhouse,' said Moominpappa, who realized that he was talking to an extraordinary person. 'I built it myself in another place, but it floated here in a great flood we had some months ago. I hope you will be happy here. I find it a very good place to work in.'

'I can work anywhere,' said the Muskrat. 'It's all a matter of thinking. I sit and think about how unnecessary everything is.'

'Really?' said Moominpappa, much impressed. 'Perhaps I might offer you a glass of wine? Against the cold?'

'Wine, I am bound to say, is unnecessary,' replied the Muskrat, 'but a small drop nevertheless would not be unwelcome.'

So Moominpappa stole into the kitchen and opened the wine-cupboard in the dark. He was stretching up for a bottle of palm-tree wine on the top shelf, stretching and stretching, when all at once there was a terrible crash: he had knocked over a vegetable-dish. In a moment the house came to life. People shouted and banged doors, and

Moominmamma came running downstairs with a candle in her paw.

'Oh! It's *you*' she said. 'I thought someone must have broken in.'

'I wanted to get the palm-tree wine down,' said Moominpappa, 'and some silly fool had put that stupid vegetable dish right on the edge of the shelf.'

'Never mind,' said Moominmamma. 'It's really a good thing it's broken – it was so ugly. Climb up on a stool dear – it will be easier.'

So Moominpappa climbed up on a stool and got down the bottle and three glasses.

'Who is the third one for?' asked Moominmamma.

'The Muskrat,' answered Moominpappa. 'A great man. He's coming to live here – with your approval, my dear.' And he called the Muskrat in and introduced him to Moominmamma.

Then they sat on the veranda and drank each other's health, and Moomintroll and Sniff were allowed down too although it was the middle of the night. It was still raining, and the wind had got trapped in the chimney and was howling eerily.

'I have lived on this river the whole of my life,' said the Muskrat, 'and never have I seen such weather. Not that it makes any difference to *me* of course, except for giving me something new to think about. It would be much better if it rained in the hot, dried-up valley on the other side of the mountains. We don't need rain here with the heavy dew we get every morning.'

'How do you know what it's like on the other side of the mountains if you've lived here all your life, Uncle Muskrat?' asked Sniff.

'An otter who swam down here once told me,' answered the Muskrat. 'I never make unnecessary journeys myself.'

'I love making journeys!' cried Moomintroll. 'There are hardly *any* unnecessary things, I think. Only eating porridge, and washing . . .'

'Hush, child,' said Moominmamma. 'The Muskrat is a wise man who knows about everything, and why it is unnecessary. I only hope, as I said, that there isn't going to be another flood.'

'Who knows?' said the Muskrat. 'There has certainly been something strange in the air lately. I have had vague forebodings and thought more than usual. It's all the same to me what happens, but one thing is certain, that *something* is going to happen.'

'Something awful?' asked Sniff, pulling his nightshirt tighter around him.

'One never knows,' said the Muskrat.

'Now we'll all go to bed,' said Moominmamma. 'It's not good for children to hear frightening stories at night.'

So they all crept into their own corners and went to sleep. But in the morning the rain clouds were still marching over the sky, and the lonely wind howled through the blue-trees.

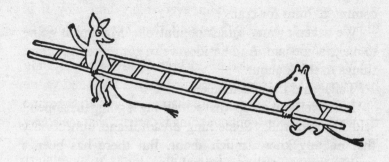

CHAPTER 2

Which is about stars with tails.

NEXT day it was cloudy. The Muskrat went out in the garden and lay in the hammock to think, and Moominpappa wrote his memoirs in the sky-blue room. Moomintroll was hanging about at the kitchen door.

'Mamma,' he said, 'do you think the Muskrat meant anything special when he mentioned those forebodings?'

'I don't think he meant so very much,' said Moominmamma. 'Don't worry about it dear. Perhaps he'd just got a chill in all that rain, and felt a bit queer. Now run along with Sniff and collect some pears from the blue-trees.'

Moomintroll went, but he was very thoughtful, and decided he would talk to the Muskrat about it later. He and Sniff carried the longest ladder they could find up the hill.

'Are we going to my cave?' asked Sniff.

'Yes,' answered Moomintroll. 'Later. But first we have to collect some pears for mamma.'

When they reached the biggest blue-tree they saw the silk-monkey sitting up in the branches waving to them.

'Hullo!' she screeched. 'What awful weather! My house

is sopping wet, and the whole forest is beastly. Are you coming to hunt for crabs?'

'We haven't time,' said Moomintroll. 'Mamma is going to make some jam. And besides we've got more important things to think about.'

'Tell!' said the silk-monkey.

'I can't tell you except that something is going to happen,' said Moomintroll. 'Something dreadful and unnecessary that nobody knows much about. But there has been a strange feeling in the air lately.'

'Ha! ha!' said the silk-monkey. 'Very funny!'

'Now shut up,' said Moomintroll putting the ladder up against the blue-tree, 'and try to be helpful for a change.'

It was great fun to pick these pears because you could throw them down as hard as you liked and they bounced off the ground like rubber balls. Moomintroll and the other two picked and threw and shouted, and the pears hopped and bounced in all directions until the ground was covered with them. The silk-monkey laughed till she nearly fell off the tree.

'That's enough,' gasped Moomintroll at last. 'We can't eat that much jam in a year. Now we'll roll the whole lot down to the river – I'll stop them at the bridge. You stay here and take care of this end, silk-monkey, and Sniff can keep an eye on the water transport.'

'Roll the pears into the river!' screamed Sniff excitedly, and he ran off to the river, while the silk-monkey rolled the pears one after another down the slope. In they plopped, swirled round in the current and bounced over the stones. Sniff ran here and there poking them with a long stick when they got caught up on their journey down to the bridge, where Moomintroll trapped them and stacked up a big pile on the bank.

After a time Moominmamma came out of the house with a big gong. 'Lunch time, children!' she cried.

'Well,' said Moomintroll, as they came up the garden, 'Haven't we picked a lot?'

'You certainly have!' exclaimed Moominmamma. 'I've never seen so many pears!'

'Then can we take our lunch out?' said Moomintroll. 'To a secret place we have?'

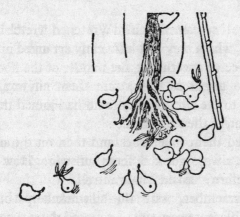

'Oh, please!' entreated Sniff. 'With lots of food so that there's enough for the silk-monkey. And could we have lemonade too?'

'Yes, of course, dears,' said Moominmamma, and she wrapped up all kinds of good things and put them in a basket, with an umbrella on top to be on the safe side.

The weather was still dull and grey when they reached the cave. Moomintroll had been rather quiet on the way up, worrying about his pearls, and directly they had crept through the opening he shouted out in alarm: 'Someone has been here!'

'In my cave!' screamed Sniff. 'Wretched wretch!'

The pearls, which they had left neatly arranged in rows, had been collected together in the middle of the floor in a pattern. 'You might as well count them anyway,' said Moomintroll to the silk-monkey, who had joined them in the wood, 'you're the treasurer.'

She counted them four times and then once more for luck, but she always got a different answer. 'How many were there before?' asked Moomintroll.

'I can't remember,' said the silk-monkey, 'but the answer was different every time I counted them then, too.'

'Oh,' said Moomintroll. 'Well that must be right I suppose. But I wonder who could have been here?'

They sat looking gloomily at the pattern of pearls.

'It *does* look like something,' said Sniff at last. 'A star I think.'

'With a tail,' said the silk-monkey.

Sniff looked suspiciously at her. 'I suppose it wasn't you who did it?' he said, for he remembered very well how the silk-monkey had made her curly flourish, marking the mysterious path, on all the tree-trunks.

'It could have been me,' she said. 'But this time it happens to have been someone else.'

'It could have been *any*body,' said Moomintroll, 'but never mind now. Let's eat first.'

So they unpacked pancakes, sandwiches, bananas and lemonade from their basket and divided it all into three equal parts. Then there was silence for some minutes while they all munched happily. When everything was finished they dug a hole in the sand and buried the paper and banana skins. And after that they dug another hole and buried the pearls. Then Moomintroll said:

'Now I've eaten and thought and everything is a little clearer. This star with a tail must be either a warning or a threat. Perhaps somebody is angry with us for some reason – a secret society for instance.'

'Do you think it's somewhere near?' asked Sniff, beginning to get anxious. 'It might easily be angry with *me*, mightn't it?'

'Yes – you especially,' said Moomintroll. 'That's very likely. Perhaps this is its cave you have discovered.'

Sniff went very pale and said: 'Perhaps we should go home?' Nobody took any notice of this of course; they went out on to the ledge and looked at the sea instead. It was like a huge grey silk eiderdown with white flowers on it. The flowers were sea-gulls resting on the water with their heads pointing out to sea.

Suddenly the silk-monkey began to laugh. 'Look!' she said, 'those funny sea-gulls think they're embroidery. They've just formed themselves into a big star!'

'With a tail!' exclaimed Moomintroll.

Sniff began to tremble violently. Then he took to his heels and ran along the ledge, quite forgetting that he had once been afraid of falling, across the sand, and off towards Moomin Valley. On the way he stumbled over tufts of grass and roots, got entangled with branches, fell on his nose, splashed through a stream, and arrived in the valley at last quite dizzy and exhausted. He shot like an arrow into Moominhouse.

'What is it now?' asked Moominmamma, who sat stirring the jam. Sniff crept very close to her and hid his nose in her apron. 'A secret society is after me,' he whispered. 'It's coming to get me and . . .'

'Not while I'm here,' said Moominmamma. 'Now, what about a nice saucepan to lick out?'

'I daren't,' whimpered Sniff. 'Not now. Perhaps never!' A little later on he said: 'Well, perhaps just the edge. While I'm waiting.'

When Moomintroll arrived, his mother's biggest jam pot was already full, and Sniff was just licking out the bottom of the saucepan.

'H'm,' said Moomintroll. 'Strange goings on.'

'What now?' asked Sniff, looking up anxiously from the saucepan.

'Nothing,' answered Moomintroll, who didn't want to frighten him still more. 'I'm going to talk to the Muskrat for a bit.'

The Muskrat was still lying in his hammock and thinking.

'Good-afternoon, Uncle Muskrat!' said Moomintroll. 'Do you know that things have begun to happen?'

'Nothing new in any case,' said the Muskrat.

'Oh yes,' said Moomintroll. 'Completely new. There are people in the forest making secret signs everywhere –

threats or warnings or something. When the silk-monkey and I came home a little while ago somebody had arranged mamma's jam pears in a pattern that looked like a star with a tail.'

The Muskrat looked at him with his shiny black eyes, twitched his moustache, but said nothing.

'There *is* something going on,' persisted Moomintroll. 'The sea-gulls made the same star, and so did the paths of the ants in the wood. I believe it's a secret society threatening the little animal Sniff with revenge.'

The Muskrat shook his head. 'I have every respect for your deductions,' he said, 'but you are wrong, completely and absolutely, and without any doubt.'

'Oh! Well that's a good thing,' said Moomintroll.

'Humph!' rejoined the Muskrat gloomily. 'Of course it's all the same to me. But I must admit I feel a trifle gratified that my foreboding was correct.'

'What do you mean?' asked Moomintroll. 'That something unnecessary is going to happen?'

The Muskrat brooded silently, his forehead creased with wrinkles. 'Do you know what a star with a tail means?' he asked at last.

'No,' said Moomintroll.

'It's a comet,' said the Muskrat. 'A glowing star that flashes through the empty black space beyond the sky trailing a fiery tail behind it.'

'Well, strike me pink!' exclaimed Moomintroll, and his eyes became black with terror. 'Will it come here?'

'I have not yet considered that point very deeply,' answered the Muskrat. 'Perhaps it will come – perhaps not. It's all the same to a person who knows that everything is unnecessary.'

Moomintroll looked up at the calm grey sky and thought

how everydayish it was. 'But all the same,' he muttered, 'I
don't like it. I don't like it at all.'

'Now I think I shall go to sleep,' said the Muskrat. 'Run
off and play my child. Play as long as you can.'

Moomintroll hesitated. 'Just one more thing,' he said, 'is
there anybody who knows a little more about the habits of

comets? Someone who knows if this one will hit the earth or
not?'

'Well, the Professors in the Observatory on the Lonely
Mountains ought to know that,' said the Muskrat. 'If they
know anything at all, that is. But now run away and leave
me in peace.'

Moomintroll went off deep in thought.

'What did he say?' asked Sniff who was waiting round
the corner. 'Was it really a secret society?'

'No,' said Moomintroll.

'And not one of those sky-monsters either?' asked Sniff
anxiously, 'not a scorpion or a bear?'

'No, no,' said Moomintroll, 'don't worry about it any
more.'

'But why are you looking so serious?' Sniff asked.

'I'm thinking,' said Moomintroll. 'I'm thinking about
you and me going on an expedition that will be the longest

ever had. We are going to find the Observatory on the ...ely Mountains, and look at the stars through the biggest ...lescope in the world. And we had better go as soon as possible.'

CHAPTER 3

Which is about how to manage crocodiles.

NEXT morning, before Moomintroll was even properly awake, he felt in his bones that it was going to be a special day. He sat up with a tremendous yawn, and then he remembered that this was the day he and Sniff were to start their great expedition. He ran to the window to look at the weather. It was still overcast, with the clouds hanging low over the hills, and not a leaf stirred in the garden. Moomintroll was so excited he had almost lost his fear of the comet.

'We'll find out where this nasty piece of work is, and then try to stop it coming here,' he thought. 'But I'd better keep this to myself, because if Sniff got to know he'd be so frightened that he wouldn't be of the smallest use to anybody.' Out loud he cried: 'Up you get little animal! We're starting now.'

Moominmamma had got up very early to pack their rucksacks, and was bustling to and fro with woolly stockings and packets of sandwiches, while down by the bridge Moominpappa was getting their raft in order.

'Mamma, dear,' said Moomintroll, 'we can't possibly take all that with us. Everyone will laugh.'

'It's cold in the Lonely Mountains,' said Moominmamma stuffing in an umbrella and a frying-pan. 'Have you got a compass?'

'Yes,' answered Moomintroll, 'but couldn't you at least leave out the plates – we can easily eat off rhubarb leaves.'

'As you like, my beloved Moominchild,' said his mother, unearthing the plates from the bottom of the rucksack. 'Now I think everything is ready.' And she went down to the bridge to see them off.

The raft was all ready with hoisted sail, and the silk-monkey had come down to say goodbye, but she had refused to go with them because she was afraid of water.

The Muskrat wasn't there because he didn't wish *anything* to disturb his contemplation of the uselessness of everything (and besides, he was rather annoyed with Moomintroll and Sniff, who had put a hairbrush in his bed).

'Now don't forget to keep on the right side of the river,' said Moominpappa. 'I shouldn't mind going along too,' he added rather wistfully, thinking of the adventurous journeys he had had in his youth with the little wandering Hattifatteners.

Sniff and Moomintroll hugged everyone, the painter was cast off and the raft began to float down the river.

'Don't forget to give my regards to all the house-troll relatives!' cried Moominmamma. 'The shaggy ones, you know, with round heads. And put on your woolly trousers when it's cold! The tummy powder is in the left-hand pocket of the rucksack!'

But the raft had already floated round the nearest bend,

and in front of them stretched the Unknown, wild and enticing.

It was late evening. Their rust-red sail hung loosely, and the river lay silver-grey between its shadowy banks. Not a bird sang; even the scatter-brained chaffinches, which usually twitter from morning till night, were silent.

'Not one adventure in a whole day,' said Sniff, who was taking his turn at steering now the current was slower. 'Just grey banks and grey banks and grey banks, and not even an adventure.'

'I think it's very adventurous to float down a winding river,' said Moomintroll. 'You never know what you'll meet round the next corner. You always want adventures, Sniff, and when they come you're so frightened you don't know what to do.'

'Well, I'm not a lion,' said Sniff reproachfully. 'I like small adventures. Just the right size.'

At that moment the raft floated slowly round a bend.

'Here's just the right sized adventure for you,' said Moomintroll pointing. Right in front of them lay what looked like a heap of big grey logs on a sandbank – and the logs were arranged in the secret pattern – a star with a tail!

'There it is again!' screamed Sniff.

Suddenly the logs began to move, and produced legs, and then the whole mass slid silently under the water.

'Crocodiles!' exclaimed Moomintroll, jumping to the rudder. 'Let's hope they don't chase us!'

The river seemed to be swarming with the monsters whose eyes shone pale green on its surface, and yet more of the fearful grey shadowy bodies were slithering down the muddy bank into the water.

Sniff sat in the stern, stiff with fear, and only moved when a crocodile lifted its nose beside him, when he beat it wildly over the head with an oar.

It was a terrible moment. Tails thrashed the water; giant mouths, bristling with needle-sharp teeth, snapped angrily, and the raft rocked up and down in the most alarming way.

Moomintroll and Sniff clung tightly to the mast and screamed for help, while the raft, caught by a little wind that had fortunately just got up, began to make headway

down the river. The crocodiles followed in a long line, their cruel jaws a-gape.

Sniff hid his face in his paws, while Moomintroll, who was so frightened he hardly knew what he was doing, got the woolly trousers out of the rucksack and threw them to their pursuers.

This distracted the crocodiles' attention at once. They tore at the woolly trousers and fought so furiously over them that by the time every bit was devoured Sniff and Moomintroll were miles away.

'Well, strike me pink!' exclaimed Moomintroll. 'Are you satisfied with that adventure?'

'You screamed too,' said Sniff.

'Did I?' said Moomintroll. 'I don't remember. Anyway it was a good thing mamma put in those woolly trousers.'

Darkness was closing in over the river, so after landing the raft they built a fire between the roots of a big tree, and fried pancakes for supper, which they ate, in their fingers, one by one as they came out of the frying-pan. Then they crept into their sleeping-bags and the night fell.

CHAPTER 4

Which is about the meeting with Snufkin and a terrible experience with a giant lizard.

DAY after day the world was shrouded in greyness, but it never rained. Columns of cloud rolled endlessly across the sky, and below them the earth lay waiting. Moomintroll and Sniff floated farther and farther east on their raft. They weren't used to being without sun, and became melancholy and quiet. Sometimes they had a game of poker or wrote a poem or caught a fish for the pot, but mostly they just sat watching the banks float by. Now and then Moomintroll contemplated the clouds and wondered whether he would see the comet if they divided. But they never did. Often he longed to tell Sniff about the great sky-monster that they were going out to look for, but it was too much of a risk. Sniff would only get in a panic.

Three times they saw the Hattifatteners, the little white creatures who are for ever wandering restlessly from place to place in their aimless quest for nobody knows what. Once they were fording the river in a shallow place and twice passing by in their small light boats. They seemed more restless than usual, hopping along at a great speed, but as they can neither hear nor speak it wasn't much use Sniff and Moomintroll even saying 'hullo' to them.

The banks looked different now. Silver poplars, plum-trees and oaks had disappeared, and dark trees with heavy branches stood alone on the deserted sand, while in the distance greyish-yellow mountains climbed steeply towards the sky.

'Oh dear,' sighed Moomintroll. 'Isn't this river ever going to end?'

'Shall we have a game of poker?' suggested Sniff.

Moomintroll shook his head. 'I don't feel like it,' he said.

'Then I'll tell your fortune,' Sniff persisted. 'Perhaps you've got one of those lucky stars shining on you.'

'Thanks,' said Moomintroll bitterly. 'I've had just about enough of stars. With or without tails.'

Sniff sighed deeply and sat for a long time disconsolately watching the strange landscape, with his nose between his paws. Suddenly his eye was caught by something out of the ordinary. It looked like a yellow ice cream cornet upside down, and was the first brightly coloured thing they had seen for a week. It was down by the edge of the water, and had what looked like a flag flying on top.

As Moomintroll and Sniff got nearer they heard quite unmistakable sounds of music, and it was cheerful music too. They strained their ears excitedly, drifting slowly nearer. At last they could see it was a tent, and gave a shout of joy.

The music stopped, and out of the tent came a snufkin with a mouth-organ in his hand. He had a feather in his old green hat and cried: 'Ahoy! Ship ahoy!'

Moomintroll caught hold of the rudder and the raft swung towards land.

'Off with the painter!' shouted Snufkin, hopping eagerly

43

up and down. 'Fancy that! What fun! Coming all this way just to see me!'

'Well – we didn't exactly,' began Moomintroll, clambering ashore.

'Never mind!' answered Snufkin. 'The main thing is that you're here. You'll stay the night, won't you?'

'We should love to,' said Moomintroll. 'We haven't seen a soul since we left home, and that was *ages* ago. Why in the world do you live here in this desert?'

'I'm a tramp, and I live all over the place,' answered Snufkin. 'I wander about and when I find a place that I like I put up my tent and play my mouth-organ.'

'Do you like *this* place?' asked Sniff in surprise, looking at the desolation all around them.

'Certainly I do,' said Snufkin. 'Look at that black velvet tree with the beautiful grey colours beyond; look at the mountains that are deep purple-red in the distance! And sometimes a big blue buffalo comes to look at himself in the river.'

'You aren't by any chance – er – a painter?' asked Moomintroll rather shyly.

'Or perhaps a poet?' suggested Sniff.

'I am everything!' said Snufkin, putting on the kettle. 'And you are discoverers I can see. What are you thinking of discovering?'

Moomintroll cleared his throat and felt very proud. 'Oh, everything,' he said. 'Stars for example!'

Snufkin was deeply impressed.

'Stars!' he exclaimed. 'Then I must come with you. Stars are my favourite things. I always lie and look at them before I go to sleep and wonder who is on them and how one could get there. The sky looks so friendly with all those little eyes twinkling in it.'

'The star we're looking for isn't so very friendly,' said Moomintroll. 'Quite the contrary in fact.'

'*What* did you say?' said Sniff.

Moomintroll went a bit red. 'I mean – stars in general,' he said, 'big and small, friendly and unfriendly and so on.'

'*Can* they be unfriendly?' asked Snufkin.

'Yes – ones with tails,' answered Moomintroll. 'Comets.'

At last it dawned on Sniff. 'You're hiding something from me!' he said accusingly. 'That pattern we saw everywhere, and you said it didn't mean anything!'

'You're too small to be told everything,' answered Moomintroll.

'*Too small!*' screamed Sniff. 'I must say it's a fine thing

45

to take me on an expedition of discovery and not tell me what I'm supposed to be discovering!'

'Don't take it too hard,' said Snufkin. 'Sit down Moomintroll, and tell us what it's all about.'

Moomintroll took the cup of coffee that Snufkin had given him, sat down, and proceeded to tell them everything that the Muskrat had said.

'And then I asked pappa if comets were dangerous,' he went on, 'and pappa said that they were. That they rushed

about like mad things in the black empty space beyond the sky trailing a flaming tail behind them. All the other stars keep to their courses, and go along just like trains on their rails, but comets can go absolutely anywhere; they pop up here and there wherever you least expect them.'

'Like me,' said Snufkin, laughing. 'They must be sky-tramps!'

Moomintroll looked disapprovingly at him. 'It's nothing to laugh at,' he said. 'It would be a terrible thing if a comet hit the earth.'

'What would happen then?' whispered Sniff.

'Everything would explode,' said Moomintroll, gloomily.

There was a long silence.

Then Snufkin said slowly: 'It would be awful if the earth exploded. It's so beautiful.'

'And what about us?' said Sniff.

But Moomintroll felt much braver now he had shared the secret with the others. He drew himself up and said: 'That's why we are going to look for the Observatory on the Lonely Mountains. They've got the biggest telescope in the world there, and we shall be able to find out if the comet is going to hit the earth or not.'

'What about taking my flag with us?' suggested Snufkin. 'We could put it at the masthead of your raft.'

They looked at his flag. 'The blue on top is the sky,' he went on, 'and the blue underneath is the sea. The line in between them is a road, the dot on the left is me at the moment, and the dot on the right is me in the future. Do you approve?'

'You could hardly get any more on a flag,' said Moomintroll. 'We approve!'

'But *I'm* not on it,' said Sniff.

'The dot on the left can be all of us, seen from a great height,' Snufkin said consolingly. 'And now I think we'll explore a bit before supper.'

So they set off, climbing cautiously between the rocks and prickly undergrowth.

'I just want to show you a cleft with garnets in it,' said Snufkin. 'It's not as beautiful as it *can* be of course in this dull light, but when the sun shines you ought to see it glittering.'

'Are they real garnets?' asked Sniff.

'That I don't know,' Snufkin answered, 'but anyway they're beautiful.'

He led them up through a wild ravine, silent and deserted

47

in the dim evening light, and they talked in whispers. Suddenly Snufkin paused. 'Here,' he said softly.

They bent down and looked. At the bottom of a deep narrow cleft myriads of garnets glowed dimly in the darkness, and Moomintroll thought of the black space beyond the sky with thousands of comets glittering in it.

'Oh!' whispered Sniff. 'Wonderful! Are they yours?'

'As long as I live here,' said Snufkin carelessly. 'I'm monarch of all I survey. I own the whole earth.'

'Do you think I could have some?' asked Sniff wistfully,

'I might be able to buy a yacht with them, or a pair of roller-skates,' and when Snufkin laughed and told him to take what he liked, he immediately jumped into the cleft and began to climb down. He scraped his nose, and almost lost his footing, but the thought of the garnets gave him courage, and at last, with a deep sigh and paws that trembled a little, he began to collect the shining stones. The pile grew larger and larger as he ran, trembling with excitement, farther and farther along the cleft.

'Hullo!' shouted Snufkin from the top. 'Aren't you coming up soon? It's getting cold and the dew is beginning to fall.'

'In a minute,' Sniff shouted back. 'There are such a lot left . . .' he trailed off, for he had just seen two huge red garnets shining like eyes, right at the dark end of the cleft.

Suddenly, to his horror, he realized that they *were* eyes – eyes that blinked and moved and came nearer, followed by a scaly body that rasped coldly on the stones.

Sniff gave one frantic squeak and ran like mad to the place where he had come down. Shaking all over he began to clamber up, his paws damp with fear, while below him sounded a soft threatening hiss.

'What's happened?' called Moomintroll, who could hear him coming. 'What's the hurry?'

Sniff didn't answer – he just climbed. And when they pulled him over the edge at last he collapsed exhausted in a heap.

Moomintroll and Snufkin leaned over the edge of the cleft and looked down. What they saw was enough to frighten anybody. It was a giant lizard crouching over a pile of shining garnets, like a hideous dragon guarding its beautiful treasure.

'Well, strike me pink!' exclaimed Moomintroll.

Sniff was sobbing on the ground.

'It's all over now,' said Snufkin. 'Don't cry any more Sniff.'

'The garnets,' Sniff moaned. 'I didn't get a single one.'

Snufkin sat down beside him and said kindly: 'I know. But that's how it is when you start wanting to *have* things. Now *I* just look at them, and when I go away I carry them in my head. Then my hands are always free, because I don't have to carry a suitcase.'

'The garnets would have gone in the rucksack,' said Sniff miserably. 'You don't need hands for that. It's not the same thing at all just looking at them. I want to touch them and know they're mine.'

'Never mind, Sniff. We're sure to find some more treasures,' said Moomintroll comfortingly. 'Now cheer up and get a move on. It's getting cold and creepy out here.'

So they made their way back through the darkening ravine, each one wrapped up in his own thoughts: three subdued little animals.

CHAPTER 5

Which is about the underground river and rescue
by a Hemulen.

Snufkin added gaiety to the expedition. He played songs on his mouth-organ that they had never heard before, songs from all corners of the earth, he did card tricks and showed them how to make fig-pancakes, and he told them many of his strange and wonderful adventures. The river, too, seemed more lively; it was narrower and flowed swift and strong, eddying round rocks and boulders between high banks.

Every day the blue and purple mountains came nearer, and they were so high that sometimes their tops disappeared in the heavy rolling clouds.

One morning Snufkin sat with his legs dangling in the water carving a whistle for himself. 'I remember,' he began, putting his head on one side, and Moomintroll and Sniff immediately pricked up their ears, 'I remember the land with the hot springs. The ground was covered with lava, and from under the lava came a continual rumbling. (It was the earth turning over in her sleep.) There were rocks strewn about higgledy-piggledy, and everything looked strange and unreal in the hot steamy atmosphere. I arrived there in the evening. It didn't take long to cook supper – I only had to fill a saucepan from a hot spring. Everything was bubbling and steaming and I didn't see a single living thing – not so much as a blade of grass.'

'Didn't you burn your feet?' asked Sniff.

'I walked on stilts,' Snufkin answered. 'They were wonderful for climbing, and I don't know what I should have done without them when the earth that had been asleep suddenly woke up! There was a great rumbling and roaring and a crater opened right in front of me, and belched out red flames and great clouds of ashes.'

'A volcano!' gasped Moomintroll and held his breath.

'Yes,' said Snufkin. 'It was awful, but beautiful too. And then I saw the fire spirits – lots of them – swarming up out of the earth and flying about like sparks. Of course I had to go a roundabout way to get past the volcano. It was hot too, so I went as fast as my stilts would carry me. Half-way down the mountain I came across a little stream and lay down to drink. (The water wasn't boiling in that stream, you see.) And then one of the little fire spirits floated down and fell into the water. He was nearly extinguished, but just had enough strength to cry out to me to save him.'

'And did you?' asked Sniff.

'Oh, yes. I had nothing against the creature,' said Snufkin. 'But I burnt myself on him you know. Well, there he was on dry land again, and presently he began to flare up to his normal state. He was very grateful of course, and gave me a present before he flew away.'

'What was it?' asked Sniff, in great excitement.

'A bottle of underground sun-oil,' answered Snufkin.

'It's what the fire spirits rub on to themselves when they go right down into the burning heart of the earth.'

'And can you go through fire when you've got this oil on?' asked Sniff, his eyes popping out with amazement.

'Of course you can,' Snufkin answered.

'But why didn't you say so before?' cried Moomintroll. 'Now we can all be saved. When the comet comes we just . . .'

'But I've got hardly any left,' said Snufkin sadly. 'I used most of it up on a couple of trips into the desert, and then saving things from a house on fire. I didn't know . . . There's only a little drop left in the bottle.'

'Perhaps there's enough for a little animal of, say, my size?' said Sniff.

Snufkin looked at him. 'Perhaps,' he said. 'But hardly for your tail as well. That will have to go.'

'Oh, help!' exclaimed Sniff. 'Then I'd rather be shrivelled right up.'

But Snufkin wasn't listening. He sat with wrinkled brow looking at the river. 'Listen,' he said, 'have you noticed anything different?'

'The river has a new sound,' said Sniff.

It was true. There was a dreadful roaring, and the water eddied and swirled between the rocky shores.

'Take down the sail,' ordered Snufkin, going forward to keep a look-out. The river was tearing along faster than ever like a person who has been out on a long journey and suddenly notices that he is late getting home for supper. The banks closed in, squeezing the foaming water into a narrow trough, and the rocks towered over them higher and steeper than ever.

'Wouldn't it be better to land?' screamed Sniff above the noise of the water.

'It's too late now,' Moomintroll screamed back. 'We must just go on till it gets calmer.'

But it didn't get calmer. They rushed wildly through the Lonely Mountains whose wet black walls closed in on either side, and the strip of sky above got narrower and narrower.

Somewhere in front of them there was a threatening rumble. 'We're going down-hill!' shouted Snufkin. 'Hold tight!'

They all held on to the mast and shut their eyes. There was a crash, a roar and a shower of spray.... Then all was quiet – they had cleared the waterfall.

'Well, strike me pink!' exclaimed Moomintroll.

It was quite dark all round them, except for patches of white-green foam, and when their eyes got used to the darkness they saw that the mountain walls had closed over them completely – they were in a tunnel!

The tunnel stretched away in front of them getting smaller and smaller; it was like a nightmare, and though the water was calmer now it was terribly dark.

'This wasn't the idea exactly,' said Moomintroll. 'We seem to be going right down into the earth, instead of up to the top of the mountains.'

They all realized the truth of this and sat for a time in gloomy silence. Then Snufkin said:

'You could write a poem about this. What about:

> Floating on this eerie water,
> Far away from bricks and mortar,'

'Saw a mermaid – didn't caught her,' suggested Sniff, blowing his nose.

'That's not true, not grammar, and it doesn't even rhyme properly,' said Snufkin, and the subject dropped.

The tunnel curved once or twice, getting even narrower and darker, and now and then the raft bumped against the walls. They picked up their rucksacks and waited. Once more there was a bump and this time the mast was knocked down.

'Snufkin,' said Moomintroll in a very small voice, 'you know what that means, don't you?'

The vault above them had become lower – or else the water had risen. Very soon it would completely fill the tunnel.

'Throw the mast overboard!' shouted Snufkin, grabbing his precious flag. 'It's no use now.'

There was another long silent wait.

It had begun to be a little lighter, and they could distinguish each other's white faces.

Suddenly Sniff shouted: 'Oh! My ears touched the roof!' and threw himself flat with a frantic squeak.

'What will mamma say,' said Moomintroll, 'if we never come home again?'

Just then the raft stopped with a thud, and they all fell together in a heap.

'We've run aground,' screamed Sniff.

Snufkin leaned over the edge and looked.

'The mast is holding us,' he said. 'It's lying across the tunnel.'

'Look what we've escaped!' said Moomintroll in a shaky voice.

Just in front of them the river disappeared with a gurgle down a black hole straight into the earth!

'I've just about had enough of voyages of discovery,' said Sniff plaintively. 'I want to go home! I suppose we'll have to sit here all our lives playing poker . . .'

'You silly little animal,' said Snufkin, 'grumbling just when we're going to be saved by nothing less than a miracle. Look up there!'

Sniff looked and saw, through a crack in the rock above them, a small patch of cloudy sky.

'Well, I'm not a bird,' he said gloomily, 'and what's more, I get dizzy fits (that's because I had inflammation of the ears when I was very young). So how could I ever get up there?'

But Snufkin took out his mouth-organ and played his gayest adventure-song (not just-the-right-sized adventure, but a terrific one) about rescues and surprises and sunshine. Moomintroll started to whistle the refrain (he couldn't sing, but he could whistle beautifully), and in the end Sniff had to join in too with his falsetto squeak. It was a bit out of tune, but fairly cheerful. Their song echoed in the tunnel and up through the crack in the roof, until it woke a Hemulen who was asleep up above, with his butterfly-net beside him.

'Whatever's that?' gasped the Hemulen with a start. He looked into his jar, where all the small creatures he had caught were imprisoned, but the insects hadn't made the noise.

It came straight out of the ground.

'Remarkable!' said the Hemulen and lay down flat to listen. 'There must be some rare caterpillar that makes that noise. I must find it.'

And he began creeping around snuffing and sniffing with his large nose, until he reached the hole in the ground where

the noise was loudest of all. He stuck his nose in as far as possible but couldn't see anything in the dark. However, the party down below saw his shadow across the light, and their song changed to a wild yell.

'Those caterpillars must have gone off their heads,' the Hemulen said to himself, pushing his net down the hole.

Of course Moomintroll and the others didn't waste much time in jumping into it with their belongings, and when the

Hemulen hauled up his heavy load and shook it out he was amazed to see three such odd creatures blinking in the daylight. '*Most* extraordinary!' he remarked.

'Thank you very much,' said Moomintroll, who pulled himself together first. 'You saved us in the nick of time.'

'Have I saved you?' asked the Hemulen in surprise. 'I didn't mean to. I was looking for the caterpillars that were making such a noise down there.' (Hemulens are generally a bit slow in grasping an idea, but they are very pleasant if you don't annoy them.)

'Are we in the Lonely Mountains now?' asked Sniff.

'I've no idea,' said the Hemulen, 'but there are plenty of interesting moths.'

'I think it *must* be the Lonely Mountains,' said Snufkin, gazing at the massive piles of rock, endless, desolate and silent, which towered on every side. The air was chilly.

'And where is the Observatory?' asked Sniff.

'We're going to look for it,' said Moomintroll. 'It's on the highest peak I believe. But first I should like to have some coffee.'

'The kettle is still on the raft,' said Snufkin.

Moomintroll loved coffee, and he rushed at once to the edge of the hole and looked down.

'Oh deary me!' he lamented. 'The raft has floated off and I suppose it's gone down that awful hole by now.'

'Well, never mind. We're not on it,' said Snufkin gaily. 'What's a kettle here or there when you're out looking for a comet!'

'Are they very rare?' asked the Hemulen who thought they were still talking about moths.

'Well, yes, I should think you could call them rare,' answered Snufkin. 'They appear about once in a hundred years.'

'No!' exclaimed the Hemulen. 'Then I must catch one. What does it look like?'

'Red probably. With a long tail,' answered Snufkin.

The Hemulen took out a notebook and wrote this down. 'It must be the Snufsigalonica family,' he said seriously. 'One more question, my learned friends, what does this remarkable insect live on?'

'On Hemulens,' said Sniff, giggling.

The Hemulen went red in the face. 'Little animal,' he said sternly, 'that is not funny. I shall now leave – with grave doubts of your scientific knowledge.' And he put his jars in his pocket, picked up his butterfly-net, and lumbered off.

Sniff doubled up with laughter when the Hemulen was out of earshot. 'How funny!' he exploded. 'The old chap thought we were talking about a beetle or something.'

'It's wrong to be disrespectful to elderly gentlemen,' said

Moomintroll severely, not, however, managing to keep a very straight face himself.

But it was getting late, so they picked out the highest mountain and set off towards it.

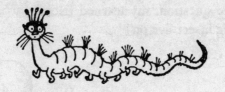

CHAPTER 6

Which is about the adventure with the Eagle and the finding of the Observatory.

IT was late evening. The age-old mountains towered into the sky, their dreaming heads lost in mist, and mist swirled in cold grey-white swathes in the chasms and valleys between. A sudden rift in the swirling vapour revealed once again the threatening sign of the comet cut by some unknown hand in a sheer wall of rock.

Just below one of the peaks could be seen a solitary pin-prick of light, and a closer look would have revealed that it was a little yellow silk tent lit up from inside. From the tent came the sound of Snufkin's mouth-organ, but in this desolate place it was a strange sound indeed. So strange that a hyena some way off, lifted up her nose and howled in the most melancholy fashion.

One member at least of the party in the tent was startled out of his wits. 'What was that?' gasped Sniff.

'Oh, nothing for you to worry about,' Snufkin reassured him. 'Listen, what about a story? Did I ever tell you about those Snorks I met a few months ago?'

'No,' said Moomintroll eagerly. 'Whatever are Snorks?'

'Don't you really know what a Snork is?' said Snufkin in amazement. 'They must be the same family as you I should think, because they look the same, except that they aren't often white. They can be any colour in the world (like an Easter egg), and they change colour when they get upset.'

Moomintroll looked quite angry. '*Well!*' he said. 'I've never heard of *that* branch of the family. A real Moomintroll is *always* white. Changing colour indeed! What an idea!'

'Well, these Snorks were very much like you anyway,' said Snufkin calmly. 'One was pale green and the other was mauve. I met them the time I escaped from prison . . . But perhaps you don't want to hear that story?'

'Oh yes! We do really,' piped Sniff, but Moomintroll only grunted.

'Well, it was like this,' began Snufkin. 'I had picked a melon for dinner. There was a whole field full of them, you see, and I thought that one more or less wouldn't make any difference. But the moment I dug my teeth into it, a nasty ugly old man came out of a house nearby, and started to shout at me. I listened for a bit, and then I began to wonder if hearing so many bad words was doing me any good. So I started rolling the melon (which was very big and heavy) along the path in front of me, whistling so that I shouldn't hear what the old man was saying. Then he shouted that the police would come after me, so I made a scornful noise to show that I wasn't afraid of the police at all.'

'How could you dare?' whispered Sniff in deep admiration.

'I really can't think,' said Snufkin. 'But now you must listen – that ugly old man *was* the police! And after dashing into his house to get into his uniform, he began to follow me. I ran and ran and the melon rolled and rolled, until in the end we were going so fast that I didn't know which was the melon and which was me.'

'And that was how you landed in prison I suppose?' said Moomintroll. 'I suppose it was there you met those creatures – Snorks didn't you call them?'

'Don't interrupt!' said Snufkin. 'I was just going to tell you how cold and horrible it was in my cell, what with the spiders and rats. I met the Snorks *outside*, after I had escaped one moonless night.'

'Did you climb out of the window with a rope made from your sheets?' asked Sniff.

'No, I dug myself out with a tin-opener,' said Snufkin. 'Twice I came up too soon, once just behind the guard and another time just inside the prison walls. But I went down and started digging again, and the third time I came up in a field. It was turnips and not melons this time, I'm sorry to say. The Snork and his sister were fishing for minnows with their tails in a nearby stream.'

'I should never *think* of fishing with my tail,' said Moomintroll. 'One should have respect for one's tail. What did you do then?'

'Oh, we celebrated my escape with minnows and cowslip wine for many hours,' answered Snufkin. 'And how beautiful the pale green Snork maiden was! She had sparkling blue eyes and was covered with beautiful soft fluff. She could weave mats of grass, and brew soothing herb drinks if you had tummy-ache. She always wore a flower behind her ear, and round her ankle she had a little gold ring.'

'Pah! Women!' scoffed Moomintroll. 'That was a rotten story. Didn't anything *exciting* happen?'

'Wasn't my escape from prison exciting enough?' said Snufkin, and went on playing his mouth-organ.

Moomintroll sniffed once more and then crept into his sleeping-bag and turned his nose to the wall.

But that night he dreamt about a little Snork maiden who looked like him, and he had given her a rose to put behind her ear.

In the morning he sat up muttering 'how silly' to himself.

The others had already begun to take down the tent, and Snufkin declared that they would reach the highest peak that day.

'But how do you know that the Observatory is on that peak especially?' asked Sniff, craning his neck to see the top, but without success as it was hidden in the clouds.

'Well,' answered Snufkin, 'you only have to look at the ground just here. It's covered with cigarette ends which have obviously been thrown out of the windows by those absent-minded scientists up there.'

'Oh, I see,' said Sniff, looking a bit crestfallen, and wishing he'd noticed the cigarette ends himself.

They began to trudge up a little twisting path, tied to each other by a rope to be on the safe side.

'Don't forget I warned you,' shouted Sniff, who was last. 'Don't blame me if something dreadful happens to us.'

Higher and higher, steeper and steeper.

'Phew!' said Moomintroll mopping his brow. 'Mamma

67

said it was cold here. Thank goodness the crocodiles ate up those woolly trousers!'

They stopped and looked down into the valley, feeling very small and lonely amongst the vast empty hills. The only living thing to be seen was an eagle circling far above them on outspread wings.

'What an enormous bird!' exclaimed Sniff. 'I feel quite sorry for him all alone in this place.'

'I expect there's a Mrs Eagle somewhere, and probably some baby eaglets too,' said Snufkin.

The bird was hovering over them, turning his head with the cold eyes and strong curved beak from side to side, when suddenly he poised himself on trembling outstretched wings.

'I wonder what he's up to now?' said Sniff.

'I don't like the look of him,' Moomintroll said anxiously.

'Perhaps . . .' began Snufkin, but he got no further, except to scream frantically: 'Look out – he's diving!'

They all threw themselves against the rocks looking wildly for somewhere to hide.

In a rush of wings the eagle swooped towards them, while they squeezed themselves into a crevice in the rock, and held each other tight in terrified helplessness. He was on top of them!

It was like a whirlwind. One moment they were surrounded by the great wings that beat wildly against the rock, and the next there was complete quiet.

Trembling in every limb they peeped out of their hiding place to see the eagle sailing in a great semi-circle below them. After a moment he rose and disappeared amongst the mountain tops.

'He's ashamed that he missed us,' said Snufkin. 'Eagles are very proud. He won't try again.'

Sniff was counting on his fingers. 'The crocodiles, the giant lizard, the waterfall, the underground tunnel, the eagle. Five awful experiences. It's beginning to get monotonous!'

'We've still got the biggest adventure to come,' said Moomintroll. 'The comet.'

They all looked up at the heavy grey clouds.

'I wish we could see the sky,' he went on rather nervously. 'Come on. Let's start!'

By the afternoon they had climbed so high that they had reached the clouds, and the going was slippery and dangerous. Damp veils of mist swirled around them. They were dreadfully cold (Moomintroll thought longingly of his woolly trousers), and surrounded completely by an awful floating emptiness.

'I always thought clouds were soft and woolly and nice to be in,' said Sniff sneezing. 'Ugh! I'm beginning to be sorry I ever came on this expedition.'

Suddenly Moomintroll stood still.

'Wait!' he said. 'There's something shining. A light . . . or is it a diamond . . .'

'A diamond!' screamed Sniff, who loved jewels.

Moomintroll set off, dragging the others after him by the rope. 'It's a little gold bracelet,' he announced at last.

'Be careful,' shouted Snufkin. 'It's right on the edge of the precipice!'

But Moomintroll wasn't listening. He crept slowly towards the edge and stretched down for the bracelet. Snufkin and Sniff held the rope tight and Moomintroll crept a little farther down until at last he reached the gold ring.

'Do you think it could be the Snork Maiden's?' he asked.

'Yes. That's hers,' said Snufkin, sighing. 'It looks as if she has fallen over the edge. So young and beautiful too.'

Moomintroll was too overcome to speak, and they went sadly on their way.

The mists were beginning to thin out and it was warmer.

70

They stopped on a ledge to rest and stared
in silence at the swirling grey vapour on
all sides of them. Suddenly it divided
and rolled away until at last the three tired
travellers could see where they were, and
what they saw took their breath away!
There was a sea of clouds at their feet,
which looked so soft and beautiful that
they wanted to wade out and dive and
dance in it.

'Now we're above the clouds,' said
Snufkin solemnly, and they turned round
to look up at the sky that had been hidden
for so long.

'Look!' whispered Sniff in terror. The
sky was no longer blue. It was a pale red!

'Perhaps it's the sunset,' said Snufkin
doubtfully.

But Moomintroll looked very grave and
said: 'No. This time it's the comet. It's
on its way to the earth.'

On the very top of the jagged peak above them stood
the Observatory. Inside, scientists made thousands of
remarkable observations, smoked thousands of cigarettes,
and lived alone with the stars.

They made their way up to it in silence and Moomintroll

opened the door. There was a staircase inside, and up they went to find themselves on the threshold of a high room with a glass roof. In the middle of the floor was a giant telescope, which revolved slowly, keeping watch on the sky, and there was the constant whirring sound of a machine. Two professors bustled here and there, tightening screws, pushing knobs and making notes.

Moomintroll gave a respectful cough. 'Good afternoon!' he said. But the scientists took no notice.

'Fine weather!' said Moomintroll a little louder. But there was still no answer. Then he went forward and touched one of the professors timidly on the arm.

'We've come several hundred miles in order to meet you, sir,' he said.

'What! You again!' exclaimed the professor.

'Excuse me,' said Moomintroll, 'but I've never been here before.'

'Then it was a couple extraordinarily like you,' muttered the professor. 'Crowds of people coming here ... We haven't time, you know, simply haven't time. This comet is the most interesting thing in the last ninety-three years. Now, what do you want? Make it quick!'

'I only w-wanted to know ... those people who were here before,' stammered Moomintroll. 'I suppose it wasn't a little pale green Snork maiden ... all fluffy ... perhaps with a flower behind her ear ...'

'Your explanation is most unscientific,' said the professor impatiently. 'I know nothing about it, except that there was a tiresome female here disturbing me about some trinket she had lost. Off with you now! You've already wasted 44 seconds of my time!'

Moomintroll backed out nervously.

'Well?' said Sniff. 'Is it coming?'

'When will it fall?' asked Snufkin.

'Oh! I quite forgot to ask,' mumbled Moomintroll blushing. 'But that little S-snork maiden has b-been here. She's alive. She didn't fall down the precipice!'

'Well, I *must* say!' Snufkin burst out.

'I can't make you out,' said Sniff. 'I thought you didn't like girls. Now *I'll* go and ask.' And he trotted up to the other professor. 'Please may I have a look through your telescope?' he asked politely. 'I am very interested in comets, and I've heard so much about your wonderful discoveries here.'

The professor was very flattered and put his spectacles

up on his forehead. 'Have you now?' he said. 'Then you must come and have a look, my little friend.'

He arranged the telescope for Sniff and told him to go ahead. Sniff was rather frightened at first. The sky was quite black and the big stars flickered as if they were alive, and far in the distance shone something red, like a wicked eye.

'Is that the comet?' he whispered.

'Yes,' said the professor.

'But it's not moving at all,' said Sniff in a puzzled voice. 'And I don't see any tail either.'

'Its tail is behind,' explained the professor. 'It is rushing straight *towards* the earth, that's why it doesn't look as if it's moving. But you can see that it gets bigger every day.'

'When will it arrive?' asked Sniff, staring in fascinated curiosity at the little red spark through the telescope.

'According to my reckoning it should hit the earth on the seventh of October at 8.42 p.m. Possibly four seconds later,' said the professor.

'And what will happen then?' asked Sniff.

'What will happen?' said the professor in surprise. 'Well, I hadn't thought about that. But I shall record the events in great detail you may be sure.'

'Can you tell me what the date is today, sir?' Sniff asked.

'It is the third of October,' answered the professor. 'And the time is exactly 6.28.'

'Then I think we must go,' said Sniff. 'Thank you very much indeed for your help.'

He returned to the others with an important look on his face.

'I have had a very interesting conversation with the

75

professor,' he said, 'and we have come to the conclusion that the comet will fall on the seventh of October at 8.42 p.m. Possibly four seconds later.'

'Then we must hurry home as fast as we can,' said Moomintroll anxiously. 'If only we can get home to mamma before it comes nothing can happen. She will know what to do.'

They left the Observatory and set off on the long journey home.

It was getting dark and the awful red light in the sky was stronger. The clouds had gone, and far down in the valley below they could just make out the narrow ribbon of the river and patches of forest.

'I'm longing to get away from this stony country,' said Snufkin. 'Even a poet can have enough sometimes.'

'I wonder where the Snorks spent the night,' said Moomintroll. 'I must give that wretched girl her ankle-ring back.' And he hurried on at such a speed that the others could hardly keep up with him.

CHAPTER 7

Which is about how Moomintroll rescues the Snork Maiden from a poisonous bush and in which the comet appears in the sky.

THE fourth of October dawned clear, but there was a strange haze over the sun as it rose slowly over the mountain-tops and sailed across the red sky. They hadn't set up the tent for the night, but had kept going all the time.

Sniff had got a blister on one foot and was grumbling.

'Well, walk on the other foot,' said Snufkin, but this wasn't very helpful advice, and at last Sniff couldn't stand it any longer.

'Oh!' he moaned. 'Now I feel giddy.' And he lay down and refused to go any farther.

'We're in a hurry,' said Moomintroll. 'I must find that little Snork as quickly as poss . . .'

'I know, I know,' interrupted Sniff. 'Your wretched Snork maiden. But that's nothing to do with me. I feel terrible, and I think I'm going to be sick.'

'We could wait a bit, couldn't we?' said Snufkin. 'And I know something we can do meanwhile. Have you ever rolled stones?'

'No,' said Moomintroll.

First Snufkin found a heap of great boulders. 'You take a

boulder,' he said, 'like this. Roll it as hard as you can over the edge of the precipice – like this. And it rushes down,' he puffed. 'Like that!'

Together they looked over the edge and watched the stone. It crashed its way down, carrying a shower of small stones with it, and for a long time the echo rumbled back and forth between the mountains.

'That was great fun!' burst out Moomintroll. 'Let's do another!' And they rolled another huge boulder on to the edge, where it balanced precariously.

'Heave ho!' shouted Snufkin. 'Heave and – push!'

Away thundered the boulder, but, oh horror, Moomintroll didn't have time to draw back and before anyone realized what was happening he was over the edge, and falling swiftly in the wake of the boulder.

Now there would very likely be one Moomintroll less in the world if he had not had a rope tied round his middle. Snufkin threw himself on the ground and braced himself for the shock. And it was a big one; Snufkin felt as if he would be cut in half.

Moomintroll swung to and fro on the end of the rope – and he was heavy.

Snufkin was dragged slowly nearer and nearer to the edge. Behind him too the rope was pulled tight, and Sniff, who was tied to the other end, began to get pulled along. 'Stop it!' he shouted. 'Leave me alone – I'm ill!'

'You'll be still worse in a minute if you don't hold on to that rope,' said Snufkin.

And then Moomintroll's voice bellowed up from below: 'Help! Pull me up!'

At last Sniff realized what was happening, and he was so frightened that he forgot to be ill. He began struggling frantically against the pulling rope, which got thoroughly

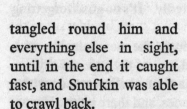

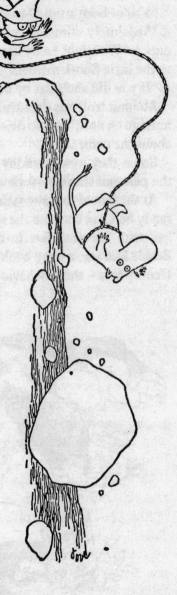

tangled round him and everything else in sight, until in the end it caught fast, and Snufkin was able to crawl back.

'When I say "*Now*" pull,' he told Sniff. 'Not now. Not now. But NOW!' And they pulled with all their might, until at last Moomintroll appeared over the edge. First his ears, then his eyes, then his nose (then still more nose) and eventually the whole of him.

'Well, strike me pink!' he exclaimed. 'I never thought I should see you two again.'

'And you never would have done, but for me,' remarked Sniff complacently. Snufkin gave him a queer look, but didn't say anything, and they all sat down to recover themselves.

'We've been stupid,' said Moomintroll suddenly.

'*You've* been stupid,' said Sniff.

'Absolutely criminal,' went on Moomintroll, taking no notice. 'We might easily have rolled one of those stones on to the little Snork maiden.'

'If you did she's flat by now,' said Sniff quite unmoved.

Moomintroll was dreadfully worried. 'Well, anyhow, we must go on now,' he said dejectedly. 'It's no good forgetting about the comet.'

So on they went, steadily down the mountainside, with the pale sun shining overhead, out of the pale red sky.

At the foot of the mountain a clear, shallow stream with a sandy bed, ran between the stones, and there sat the Hemulen, with his tired feet in the water, sighing to himself. Beside him was a large book called: 'Moths of the Eastern Hemisphere – their Behaviour and Misbehaviour.'

'Extraordinary!' he was muttering. 'Not one with a red tail. It might have been Dideroformia Archimboldes, but that is very common and has no tail at all.' And he sighed again.

Just then Moomintroll, Snufkin and Sniff popped out from behind a rock and said 'Hullo!'

'Oh! How you frightened me!' gasped the Hemulen. 'So it's only you three again. I thought it was another avalanche. This morning it was terrible.'

'What was?' asked Sniff.

'The avalanche of course,' answered the Hemulen. 'Quite terrible! Rocks the size of houses bouncing about like hail-stones! My best glass jar was broken, and I myself had to move quite quickly to get out of the way.'

'I'm afraid we happened to knock a few stones down as we were passing,' said Snufkin. 'It's so easily done walking on these tracks.'

'Do you mean to say it was *you* who made the avalanche?' said the Hemulen.

'Well – yes – sort of,' Snufkin answered.

'I never thought very much of you,' said the Hemulen slowly, 'and now I think even less. In fact I don't think I want to know you any more.' And he turned away and splashed some water over his tired feet. Snufkin and the others didn't quite know what to say, so they kept silent. After a while the Hemulen looked over his shoulder and remarked: 'Haven't you gone yet?'

'We're just going,' said Moomintroll. 'But first I feel it's my duty to ask you if you haven't noticed something odd about the colour of the sky?'

'The colour of the *sky*?' asked the Hemulen, innocently.

'Yes,' said Moomintroll, 'that's what I said.'

'Why ever should I?' said the Hemulen. 'It can be

spotted for all I care. I hardly ever look at it. What worries *me* is that my beautiful mountain stream is nearly dried up. If it goes on like this much longer I shan't be able to splash my feet.'

And he turned away again, muttering and growling to himself.

'Come on,' said Moomintroll. 'I think he'd rather be alone.'

The ground was getting softer to walk on. It was thick with lichen and moss, and a few shy flowers peeped out here and there, while below them the dark carpet of the forest looked quite near.

'We'll make straight for this flowering valley of yours,' said Snufkin, 'because we *must* get there before the comet comes.'

Moomintroll looked at his compass. 'I think there's something wrong with this thing,' he said, 'it's dancing about like a midge over water.'

'It's the comet's fault, I expect,' said Sniff.

'We shall have to go by the sun,' said Snufkin, 'though *it* doesn't seem to be much use either just now.'

A little farther down they came to a tarn, which had sunk so low in its stone basin that the sides were too steep for them to get down and have a swim. There was a rim of weeds and rushes some feet above the water level, and it was still wet.

'Funny,' said Snufkin with wrinkled forehead, 'the water sinking as much and as quickly as that.'

'There must be a hole in the bottom,' said Sniff, 'for the water to run out of.'

'The Hemulen's stream had sunk too,' said Moomintroll.

Sniff looked anxiously into their lemonade bottle, but to his relief that seemed to have as much in it as before.

'I can't understand it,' he said.

'Never mind, Sniff,' said Moomintroll. 'Perhaps it's better if you can't. Come on now!'

Just then they heard a cry for help.

It came from the wood just ahead of them, and they set off at top speed to the rescue.

'All right!' shouted Snufkin. 'We're coming!'

'Not so fast!' panted Sniff. 'Ow!' for he had fallen over, and was being dragged along on his nose by the rope, which still tied the three of them together. But the others didn't stop until they too were brought up nose to nose on each side of a tree, with the rope hooked across its trunk.

'Darned rope!' Moomintroll said angrily.

Sniff was shocked. 'Oh!' he gasped, 'you swore!'

Moomintroll ignored him, and hacking at the rope with his knife, muttered something about it being the Snork maiden who had called. The moment he was free he set off again as fast as his short legs would carry him.

The next minute the Snork came panting up, green with terror. (Snufkin didn't recognize him at first, because, as you may remember, the Snork was mauve when they had met before.)

'Hurry!' he screamed. 'My sister! A terrible bush! It's eating her up!'

And to their horror they found that this was actually the case. A poisonous bush of the dangerous Angostura family had got hold of the little Snork maiden's tail, and was now dragging her towards it, while she uttered shrill cries and struggled with all her might.

'Miserable bush!' cried Moomintroll and, brandishing

his pen-knife (the new one with a corkscrew and an instrument-for-taking-the-stones-out-of-horses'-hooves), he circled round it shouting rude names, such as 'earth-worm,' 'scrubbing-brush' and 'rat-tailed pest'. The bush glared at Moomintroll with all its greeny-yellow flower-eyes, and at last let go of the Snork maiden and stretched its twining arms towards him instead. Snufkin and the others watched the wild battle that followed hardly daring to breathe.

Moomintroll lunged about, with his tail beating angrily, and all the time he attacked the Angostura's waving arms.

A howl of terror was heard from the spectators when one of the green arms twisted itself round Moomintroll's nose. But it changed to a triumphal war-cry when he chopped off the arm with a single blow. Then the fight became more violent; the bush was trembling all over, and Moomintroll was quite red in the face with fury and effort. For a long time you could see nothing but a whirl of arms, tail and legs.

The Snork maiden found a big stone, which she threw into the middle of the fight, but as the stone hit Moomintroll in the tummy it didn't help much.

'Oh dear! Oh dear!' moaned the Snork maiden, 'I've killed him!'

'Just like a girl!' said Sniff.

But Moomintroll wasn't dead yet. He came up fighting harder than ever and cut off one after another of the Angostura's arms. When nothing but a tree-stump was left he folded up his knife and said – in a rather superior manner, Sniff thought – 'Well! That's that!'

'Oh, how brave you are!' whispered the Snork maiden.

'Oh, I do that sort of thing nearly every day,' said Moomintroll airily.

'Do you?' said Sniff. 'I've never . . .' But he got no farther than a squeak because Snufkin had trodden on his toe.

'What was that?' asked the Snork maiden with a start, because she was rather nervous after her dreadful experience.

'Don't be frightened,' said Moomintroll. 'I'm here to protect you. I've got a little present for you too,' and he produced the gold ankle-ring.

'Oh!' exclaimed the Snork maiden, turning quite pink with pleasure. 'I thought I'd lost it. Oh, how wonderful!' She put the ring on at once, and then turned and twisted, trying to see the effect.

'She's been fussing about that ring for two days,' said the Snork. 'She could hardly eat. And now, if you are all willing, I suggest we go on to a little glade that I know, and hold a meeting. I think we have more important things than rings to discuss.' So the Snork led them to his glade and there they sat in a circle and waited.

'Well,' said Moomintroll, 'what are we going to talk about?'

'About the comet, of course,' answered the Snork, glancing fearfully at the red sky. 'First of all I elect myself president and secretary of this meeting. Are there any objections?' Nobody had any objections, and the Snork tapped the ground three times with his pencil. The Snork maiden thought he was killing an ant.

'Was it a poisonous one?' she asked with interest.

'Hush! You're disturbing the meeting!' said her brother. 'It will fall on the seventh of October at 8.42 p.m. Perhaps four seconds later.'

'What? the poisonous ant?' asked Moomintroll, who was a bit mixed up, what with the battle with the bush and the Snork maiden's beauty.

'No, no, the comet,' said the Snork impatiently. 'Now we must ask ourselves what should be done?'

'We thought we'd go home as quickly as possible,' said Moomintroll. 'I hope you and your sister will come with us.'

'I shall have to think it over,' answered the Snork. 'We

can go more deeply into the question at the next meeting.'

'Listen,' interrupted Snufkin, 'this has got to be decided at once. It's the fourth of October today, and it's already afternoon. We have exactly three days to reach Moomin Valley.'

'Do you live there?' asked the Snork maiden.

'Yes,' said Moomintroll. 'It's a wonderful valley. And just before we left I made a swing, and Sniff has discovered a magnificent cave that I shall show you . . .'

'Wait a minute,' said the Snork, tapping the ground again, 'keep to the point please. Now is it possible for us to reach there before the comet, and if so can we be safe in this valley of yours?'

'It's been all right up to now,' said Sniff.

'Mamma will think of something,' said Moomintroll. 'You must see the cave where I've buried my pearls!'

'Pearls!' burst out the Snork maiden excitedly. 'Could ankle-rings be made out of pearls?'

'I should just think they *could*,' said Moomintroll. 'Ankle-rings and nose-rings and ear-rings and engagement rings . . .'

'That's a question for later,' the Snork cut in, thumping furiously with his pencil. 'Be quiet now! My dear sister, there *are* more important things in the world than nose-rings.'

'Not if they're made of pearls,' said the Snork maiden. 'Now you've broken the point of your pencil again. Doesn't anybody want to eat this evening?'

'Yes, I do!' shouted Sniff.

'We will adjourn the meeting until tomorrow morning,' said the Snork with a sigh. 'There's never any order when girls are about.'

'Don't take it so seriously,' said his sister, and began to

87

take plates out of a little basket. 'It would be much better if you collected some wood for me. Besides we shall be quite safe in this cave in Moomin Valley, so what are you worrying about?'

'Why, what a wonderful idea!' exclaimed Moomintroll, looking at her in admiration. 'How clever of you to think of it. Of course! We can hide in the cave when the comet comes!'

'In *my* cave,' squeaked Sniff proudly. 'We'll roll stones across the opening, and cover the hole in the roof, and take lots of food down there, and a lantern. Won't it be exciting?'

'Well, now we'll have to have a meeting anyway,' said the Snork. 'We must organize a working party.'

'Yes, yes,' said his sister impatiently. 'How about that wood? And, Sniff, will you go and fetch some water from the marsh please?'

Sniff and the Snork set off and the Snork maiden went on laying the table. 'Moomintroll, will you pick some flowers for the table?' she said.

'What colour would you like?' he asked.

The Snork maiden looked at herself and saw that she was still pink. (This had come over her when Moomintroll gave back the ring, you remember.) 'Well,' she said, 'I think blue flowers would suit me best.' So Moomintroll trotted off to find some.

'And what can *I* do?' asked Snufkin.

'Play something for me please!' said the Snork maiden.

So Snufkin took out his mouth-organ and played a song about the blue horizon.

It was a long time before the Snork came back with the wood. 'Well, there you are at last,' said his sister.

'It took quite a time,' said the Snork, 'because of course I had to find pieces that were all exactly the same length.'

'Is he always so particular?' asked Snufkin.

'He was born like that,' said the Snork maiden. 'Where's Sniff with that water?'

But Sniff hadn't found any water. The marsh was dried up; only a little mud lay at the bottom, and all the poor water-lilies had died. He went farther into the wood and found a stream, but that was dry too. It was most extraordinary. At last Sniff returned crest-fallen to the camp.

'I think all the water in the world must have dried up,' he said.

'We must discuss the matter,' said the Snork. But his sister had a better idea. 'Sniff, didn't you have a bottle of lemonade?' she asked, and when he brought one out she emptied it into the saucepan with some berries, and produced the most wonderful fruit-soup that you could imagine.

'But soup isn't the only thing we have to worry about,' said the Snork thoughtfully. 'There must be some reason why all the water has dried up.'

'It's probably because the sun is so hot,' said Snufkin.

'Or else the comet,' said Sniff, and they all looked up at the sky. It was a dull red in the gathering darkness, and there, just above the tree-tops, something shone. A little

red spark like a distant star. It didn't move, but it seemed to flicker and burn as if it were very hot.

The Snork maiden shivered and crept nearer to the fire. 'Oh dear,' she said, 'it doesn't look very friendly.' And her colour slowly changed from pink to mauve.

While they sat and looked at the comet Moomintroll came puffing up with a bunch of bluebells. 'It wasn't very easy to find them,' he said.

'Thank you very much,' said the Snork maiden, 'but I should really have asked for yellow flowers – you see I've changed colour again!'

'Oh, deary me!' said Moomintroll sadly. 'Shall I find you some others?' And then he too caught sight of the comet shining over the tree-tops.

'No, no, don't bother,' answered the Snork maiden, 'but please hold my paw! I'm frightened!'

'You mustn't be,' comforted Moomintroll. 'We know it won't hit the earth for three days, and by that time we shall be home, and snug in the cave. Now we'll eat your marvellous soup and then go to sleep.'

So the Snork maiden ladled out the soup, and when they had eaten they all curled up together on the mat which she had woven out of grass.

The fire slowly died – but above the dark silent wood the comet shone red and ominous.

CHAPTER 8

*Which is about the Village Stores and a party
in the forest.*

THE whole of the next day they travelled through the wood, straight towards Moomin Valley, and Snufkin went in front playing his mouth-organ to keep their spirits up. At about five o'clock in the afternoon they came to a little path which had a big notice beside it, with an arrow, saying:

DANCING TO-NIGHT
This way!
VILLAGE STORES

'Oh, I want to dance! *Couldn't* we dance?' cried the Snork maiden, clapping her paws. 'I haven't been dancing for ages and ages.'

'We haven't time for that sort of thing now,' said the Snork.

'Perhaps we could buy some lemonade at that village stores,' said Sniff. 'I'm so thirsty.'

'Anyway the path goes in exactly our direction,' said Moomintroll.

'We could just have a look at the dancing as we go by,' suggested Snufkin.

The Snork sighed. 'You're quite hopeless all of you,' he said with a resigned air.

It was a funny little path, winding here and there, dashing off in different directions, and sometimes even tying a knot in itself from sheer joy. (You don't get tired of a path like that, and I'm not sure that it doesn't get you home quicker in the end.)

Snufkin cut a flag pole and hoisted his precious flag once again. Sniff carried it while Snufkin played, and the Snork maiden frisked in and out between the trees picking flowers to match whatever mood she happened to be in, and putting them behind her ears.

'Tell me some more about your valley,' she said to Moomintroll.

'It's the most wonderful valley in the world,' he answered. 'There are blue-trees with pears growing on them, and chatterfinches sing from morning till night, and there are plenty of silver poplars, which are wonderful for climbing – I thought of building a house for myself in one of them. Then, at night the moon is reflected in the river, which tinkles over the rocks with a sound like broken glass, and pappa has built a bridge that is wide enough for a wheelbarrow.'

'Must you be so poetic?' said Sniff. 'When we were in the valley you only talked about how wonderful other places were.'

'That was different,' said Moomintroll.

'But it's true,' said Snufkin. 'We're all like that. You must go on a long journey before you can really find out how wonderful home is.'

'Where's *your* home then?' asked the Snork maiden.

'Nowhere,' said Snufkin a little sadly, 'or everywhere. It depends on how you look at it.'

'Haven't you got a mother?' asked Moomintroll looking very sorry for him.

'I don't know,' said Snufkin. 'They tell me I was found in a basket.'

'Like Moses,' said Sniff.

'I like the story about Moses,' said the Snork. 'But I think his mother could have found a better way of saving him don't you? The crocodiles might have eaten him up.'

'They nearly ate us up,' said Sniff.

'Moses' mother could have hidden him in a box with air-holes,' said the Snork maiden. 'That would have kept the crocodiles out.'

'Once we tried to make a diving helmet with an air-tube,' said Sniff. 'But we could never get it really water-tight. Once when Moomintroll was diving he swallowed some water and nearly choked. It *was* funny!'

'Oh!' exclaimed the Snork maiden in horror. '*I* think it must have been awful.'

As they were wandering along and talking like this they suddenly came in sight of the Village Stores. Sniff gave a shout and waved the flag over his head, and they all hurried excitedly up the path.

It was a really good Village Stores. The garden had all the flowers you can think of planted in neat rows, and the house was white with grass growing on the roof. In front was a kind of sundial, but instead of telling the time it held a big silver ball like a looking glass, and in this the house and garden were reflected.

There were signs and posters for soap, and toothpaste, and chewing gum, and under the window grew huge yellow and green pumpkins.

Moomintroll went up the steps and opened the door, which set a little bell tinkling over his head. They trooped in, one after another, all except the Snork maiden, who stayed out in the garden admiring herself in the silver ball. Behind the counter sat an old lady with little bright eyes like a mouse, and white hair.

'Aha!' she said. 'What a lot of children. And what can I do for you, my dears?'

'Lemonade please ma'am,' said Sniff. 'Green if you've got it.'

'Have you an exercise book with lines one inch apart?' asked the Snork, who intended to write down everything

95

that ought to be done when a comet is going to hit the earth.

'Certainly,' said the old lady. 'Would you like a blue one?'

'Well, I'd prefer another colour,' said the Snork, because blue exercise books reminded him of school.

'I really need a new pair of trousers,' said Snufkin. 'But they needn't be *too* new. I like trousers that have stretched to my own shape.'

'Yes, of course,' said the old lady, climbing up a ladder and hooking a pair of trousers down from the roof. 'What about these?'

'But they are so horribly new and clean,' said Snufkin sadly. 'Haven't you got something older?'

The old lady thought for a time. 'These are the oldest trousers I have in stock,' she said at last, 'and tomorrow they'll be still older. Probably dirtier too,' she added looking at Snufkin over her glasses.

'Oh, well,' he said, 'I might as well go round the corner and try them on. But I very much doubt if they'll be my shape.' And he disappeared into the garden.

'Now, what about you, my dear?' said the old lady, turning to Moomintroll, who wriggled with embarrassment and asked shyly: 'Have you got such a thing as a diamond tiara?'

'A diamond tiara?' the old lady asked in surprise. 'What are you going to do with that?'

'He wants to give it to the Snork Maiden, of course,' squeaked Sniff, who was sitting on the floor drinking green lemonade through a straw. 'He's been quite dotty since he met that girl.'

'It's not dotty at all to give jewellery to a girl,' said the old lady severely. 'You are too young to understand, but as a matter of fact, a jewel is the only correct present for a lady.'

'Oh,' said Sniff, and buried his nose in the lemonade.

The old lady searched all her shelves, but there was no tiara.

'Perhaps there's one under the counter?' suggested Moomintroll.

The old lady had a look. 'No,' she said sadly, 'not there either. Fancy not having a single tiara. But perhaps a little pair of Snork-mittens would do instead?'

'I'm not quite sure . . .' said Moomintroll, looking very worried.

At that moment the door-bell tinkled and the Snork maiden herself came into the shop.

'Good afternoon,' she said. 'What a beautiful looking-glass you have out there in the garden! Since I lost my pocket one I've had to look at myself in puddles, and you look so funny in puddles.'

The old lady winked at Moomintroll, took something from a shelf and passed it to him under the counter. Moomintroll glanced down: it was a little round looking-glass with a silver rim, and on the back was a red rose studded with rubies. He was very pleased and winked back at the old lady. The Snork maiden hadn't noticed anything.

97

'Have you any medals, ma'am?' she asked.

'Any *what*, my dear?' said the old lady.

'Medals,' said the Snork maiden. 'Stars to hang on the chest. Gentlemen like such things.'

'Oh, yes, of course,' said the old lady. 'Medals.' And she looked all over the place – on all the shelves and under the counter.

'Haven't you got any?' asked the Snork maiden, and a tear began to trickle down her nose.

The old lady looked most unhappy, but she suddenly had an idea and climbed up the ladder to the highest shelf, where there was a box of Christmas-tree decorations, and amongst these she found a big silver star.

'Look!' she cried, holding it up, 'here's a medal for you!'

'Oh, how beautiful!' the Snork maiden burst out. Then she turned to Moomintroll and said shyly: 'This is for you Moomintroll. Because you saved me from the poisonous bush.'

Moomintroll was overwhelmed. He knelt down, and the Snork maiden pinned the star somewhere about his tummy (Moomintrolls' noses cover up their chests, so you can't very well pin medals there), where it shone with matchless splendour.

'Now you should see how wonderful you look,' said the Snork maiden. At this Moomintroll brought out the looking-glass that he had been holding behind his back. 'I bought this for you,' he said. 'Show me how *you* look in it!'

While they were gazing at themselves in the glass and exclaiming 'Oh', and 'Ah', the door-bell tinkled again and Snufkin came in.

'I think it would be better if the trousers got older here,' he said. 'They aren't my shape yet.'

'Oh dear,' said the old lady. 'What a pity! But perhaps you'd like a new hat?'

However this idea only filled Snufkin with alarm, and he pulled his old green hat farther down over his ears and said: 'Thank you, but I was just thinking how dangerous it is to load yourself up with belongings.'

The Snork had been sitting all this time writing in his exercise book, and now he got to his feet and said: 'One thing to remember when you are escaping from a comet is not to stand about too long in village stores. I suggest therefore that we continue our journey. Hurry up and finish your lemonade, Sniff.'

Sniff tried to gulp the lot and of course most of it went on the floor.

'He always does that,' said Moomintroll. 'Shall we go?'

'What does all that come to please?' the Snork asked the old lady. She began to count up, and while she was doing so Moomintroll suddenly remembered that they hadn't any money with them. None of them even had pockets except Snufkin, and his were always empty. Moomintroll nudged him, making desperate signs with his eyebrows, and the

Snork and his sister looked at each other in horror. Not one of them had a single penny!

'That'll be 1¾d. for the exercise book, and 3d. for the lemonade,' said the old lady. 'The star is 5d. and the looking-glass 11d. because it has real rubies on the back. That will be 1/8¾d. altogether.'

Nobody said anything. The Snork maiden picked up the looking-glass and laid it on the counter with a sigh. Moomintroll started unpinning his medal, the Snork wondered if exercise books cost more or less after you had written in them, and Sniff just thought about his lemonade, which was mostly on the floor anyway.

The old lady gave a little cough.

'Well now, my children,' she said. 'There are the old trousers that Snufkin didn't want; they are worth exactly 1/8d., so you see one cancels out the other, and you don't really owe me anything at all.'

'Is that really so?' asked Moomintroll doubtfully.

'It's as clear as day, little Moomintroll,' said the old lady. 'I'll keep the trousers.'

The Snork tried to count it up in his head, but he couldn't, so he wrote it in the exercise book like this:

	s.	d.
Exercise book		1¾
Lemonade		3
Medal		5
Looking-glass (with rubies)		11
Total	1	8¾
Trousers	1	8

1/8d. = 1/8d.
¾d. left over.

'It's quite right,' he said in surprise.

'But there's ¾d. over,' said Sniff. 'Don't we get that?'

'Don't be mean,' said Snufkin. 'We'll call it even.'

So they thanked the old lady and were just leaving when the Snork maiden remembered something. 'Can you tell us where the dancing is tonight please?' she asked.

'Well,' said the old lady, 'you just follow the path until you come to it – and nothing begins until the moon gets up.'

They had left the Village Stores some way behind when Moomintroll stopped and put his hand to his head. 'The comet!' he exclaimed. 'We must warn the old lady about it, mustn't we? Perhaps she would like to come with us and hide in the cave. Sniff, will you run back and ask her?'

Sniff trotted off, and they sat down by the side of the path to wait.

'Can you dance the samba?' the Snork maiden asked Moomintroll.

'Well, a bit,' he answered, 'but I like the waltz best.'

'We've hardly got time for this dance tonight,' said the Snork. 'Look at the sky.'

They looked.

101

'It's got bigger,' said Snufkin. 'Yesterday it was a mere pin-head. Now it's the size of an egg.'

'But I'm sure you can do the tango,' went on the Snork maiden. 'One short step to the side and two long steps backwards.'

'It sounds easy,' said Moomintroll.

'Sister,' said the Snork, 'you haven't a serious thought in your head. Can't you ever keep to the point?'

'We began talking about dancing,' said the Snork maiden, 'and then suddenly you started talking about the comet. I'm still talking about dancing.'

Then they both slowly began to change colour. But luckily Sniff ran up just then. 'She doesn't want to come with us,' he said. 'She is going to creep into the cellar when it comes. But she is very grateful and sent us a lollipop each.'

'You didn't *ask* for them by any chance?' asked Moomintroll suspiciously.

'Wretched wretch!' exclaimed Sniff indignantly. 'What an idea! She thought we ought to have them as she owed us ¾d. And after all that's quite true.'

So they went on, sucking their lollipops, while the sun sank behind the trees, shrouded in a grey mist.

The moon came up, looking rather green and pale, and the comet shone stronger than ever. It was now nearly as big as the sun and lit up the whole wood with its strange red light.

They found the dance floor in a little clearing, round which thousands of glow-worms had kindly festooned themselves. Nearby sat a giant grass-hopper with a large mug of beer in his hand, and a fiddle on the grass beside him.

'Phew!' he said. 'It's pretty warm to be playing all the time.'

'Who are you playing for?' asked the Snork maiden looking at the empty dance floor.

'Oh, the forest creatures from hereabouts,' said the grass-hopper with a sweep of his arm, and took another drink. 'But the silly little things aren't satisfied. They say my music isn't modern enough.'

Then they realized that the place was swarming with all kinds of strange little people. Even the water-spooks who had come up out of the dried up marshes and forest pools were there, and groups of tree-spirits sat gossiping under the birch trees. (A tree-spirit is a beautiful little creature who lives in a tree-trunk, but at night she flies up to the top of the tree to swing in the branches – she isn't usually found in trees that have needles instead of leaves.)

The Snork maiden picked up her looking-glass to see if the flower behind her ear looked all right, and Moomintroll put his medal straight. It was a long time since they had been to a real ball.

'I don't want to offend the grass-hopper,' whispered Snufkin, 'but do you think I could play a little for them on my mouth-organ?'

'Why don't you play together?' suggested the Snork. 'Teach him that song "All small beasts should have bows in their tails".'

'That's a good idea,' said Snufkin. And he took the grass-hopper behind a bush (it wasn't a poisonous one this time) to teach him the song.

After a while a few notes were heard, and then some trills and twiddles. All the small creatures stopped chattering and went down to the clearing to listen. 'That sounds modern,' they said. 'You can dance to that.'

'Oh, mamma!' exclaimed one very small creature, pointing at Moomintroll's star, 'there's a general!'

whereupon they all gathered round the travellers with cries of astonishment and admiration.

'How nice and fluffy you are!' they said to the Snork maiden. And the tree-spirits looked at themselves in the looking-glass with rubies on the back, and the water-spooks put their wet autographs in the Snork's exercise book.

Then there were sounds from behind the bush, and out came Snufkin and the grass-hopper playing with all their might.

There was a dreadful muddle at first while they all tried to sort each other out, but at last everybody found the person he wanted to dance with, and they started off.

The Snork maiden taught Moomintroll how to dance the samba (which isn't at all easy if you have very short legs). The Snork danced with an elderly and respectable inhabitant of the marshes, who had sea-weed in her hair, and Sniff twirled round with the smallest of the small creatures. Even the midges danced, and every possible kind of creeping thing came out of the forest to have a look.

And nobody gave a thought to the comet that was rushing towards them, lighting up the black night with its fierce glow.

At about twelve o'clock a huge barrel of palm-wine was rolled out, and everybody got a little birch-bark mug to drink out of. Then the glow-worms rolled themselves together into a ball in the middle of the glade, and everybody sat round drinking wine and eating sandwiches (which had also been provided).

'Now we should tell a story,' said Sniff, turning to the smallest of the small creatures, 'do *you* know one, Little Creep?'

'Oh, no, really,' whispered the Little Creep, who was terribly shy. 'Oh, no, well, really, perhaps.'

'Well, out with it then,' said Sniff.

'There was a wood-rat called Poot,' said the Little Creep, looking shyly between her paws.

'Well, what happened then?' prompted Sniff.

'The story's finished now,' said the Little Creep, and burrowed into the moss in confusion.

They all roared with laughter, and those who had tails beat them on the ground in appreciation. Then Moomintroll asked Snufkin for a song.

'We'll take the Higgely-piggely song,' he said.

'But that's so sad,' protested the Snork maiden.

'Well, let's have it anyway,' said Moomintroll, 'because it's such a good whistling song.' So Snufkin played and everybody joined in with the refrain:

> Higgely-piggely,
> Path is so wiggely,
> Time is past four.
> Almost dead beat
> On tired little feet;
> No friendly door.

The Snork maiden leant her head on Moomintroll's shoulder. 'It's just what has happened to us,' she sobbed.

'Here we are almost dead-beat on tired little feet, and we shall never get home.'

'Yes, we shall,' said Moomintroll, 'don't cry. And when we get there Mamma will have dinner ready and she'll take us in her arms, and think what fun it will be to tell them all about what has happened to us.'

'And I shall have a pearl ankle-ring,' said the Snork maiden, drying her tears. 'And what about a pearl tie-pin for you?'

'Yes,' said Moomintroll, 'that would be nice, but then I hardly ever wear a tie.' The Snork maiden couldn't think of an answer to this, so they stopped talking, and listened to Snufkin who was still playing his mouth-organ. He played one song after another, until gradually all the little animals and water-spooks faded back into the wood. The tree spirits crept into their trees, and the Snork maiden went to sleep with her looking-glass in her paw.

At last the songs were ended and it was quite still in the glade. The glow-worms went out one by one, and very slowly the night crept towards morning.

CHAPTER 9

*Which is about a fantastic crossing of the dried-up sea and how
the Snork Maiden rescues Moomintroll from
a giant octopus.*

On the fifth of October the birds stopped singing. The sun
was so pale that you could hardly see it at all, and over the
wood the comet hung like a cartwheel, surrounded by a ring
of fire.

Snufkin didn't play his mouth-organ that day. He was
very quiet and thought to himself, 'I haven't felt so depres-
sed for a long time. I usually feel sad, in a way, when a good
party is over, but this is something different. It's horrible
when the sun has gone and the forest is silent.'

The others hadn't much to say either. Sniff had a head-
ache and was grumbling to himself. Their feet were tired
after so much dancing, and progress was a bit slow.

Gradually the trees thinned out, and by and by a landscape of deserted sand-dunes lay before them: nothing but
soft sandy hillocks with here and there tufts of blue-grey
sea-oats.

'I can't smell the sea,' said Moomintroll, sniffing. 'Phew! It's hot.'

'Perhaps this is a desert,' said Sniff.

On and on they went, up one hill and down another, and it was heavy going on the soft sand.

'Look!' said the Snork suddenly. 'The Hattifatteners are on the move again.' And sure enough there in the distance was a wavering line of little figures.

'They're going east,' said the Snork. 'Perhaps we'd better follow them, because they always know where danger lies and try to get away from it.'

'But we *must* go this way,' said Moomintroll. 'The Valley is to the west.'

'I'm so thirsty,' wailed Sniff.

But nobody answered.

Tired and discouraged they struggled on. The sand-dunes gradually got flatter and flatter, and then stopped at a line of sea-weed glistening in the red light. Beyond this was a pebbly beach – and then ... They stood in a row and stared!

'Well, strike me pink!' said Moomintroll.

Where the sea should have been, with soft blue waves and friendly sails, there gaped a yawning abyss.

Hot steam rose from the depths of great cracks that seemed to go down to the very heart of the earth, and below them the cliff went down ... down ...

'Moomintroll!' gasped the Snork maiden. 'The whole sea has dried up.'

'What *will* the fishes say to that?' exclaimed Sniff.

The Snork took out his exercise book, and added something to the list headed: 'Risks encountered during Approach of Comet,' but Snufkin sat down with his head in his hands and wailed: 'Oh, dear, oh, dear, the beautiful sea

quite gone. No more sailing, no more swimming, no more fishing. No great storms, no transparent ice and no gleaming black water reflecting the stars. Finished, lost, gone!' And he put his head on his knees and cried as if his heart would break.

'But Snuff,' said Moomintroll reproachfully, 'you have always been so happy-go-lucky. It's dreadful to see you despairing like this.'

'I know,' said Snufkin. 'But I've always loved the sea more than anything else. This is so sad.'

'Especially for the fish,' squeaked Sniff.

'What seems to be most important,' said the Snork, 'is how we are going to get across this huge gap, because we haven't got time to go round it.'

'No, of course not,' Moomintroll agreed anxiously.

'Let's hold a meeting,' said the Snork. 'I will take the

chair. Now, what alternatives have we for crossing a dried-up sea?'

'Flying,' said Sniff.

'Don't be silly,' said the Snork. 'Proposal rejected. Unanimously. Well?'

'Walking,' suggested Moomintroll.

'You *are* stupid,' said the Snork. 'We should fall down those great cracks, or sink into the mud. Proposal rejected.'

'Propose something yourself then!' said Moomintroll angrily.

Then Snufkin lifted his head. 'I know,' he cried, 'stilts!'

'Stilts?' said the Snork. 'Proposal re . . .'

'Wait a minute,' cried Snufkin. 'Listen. Don't you remember how I used stilts in the land of the hot springs? In one stride I could get over practically anything. It's quick too.'

'But isn't it awfully difficult to walk on stilts?' asked the Snork maiden.

'You can practice here on the beach,' answered Snufkin. 'Now it's only a question of finding stilts.'

So they all set off in different directions on a stilt-hunt, and it wasn't a very easy hunt either.

The Snork faced the problem most sensibly. He thought: Stilts are long poles. What are poles? They are tree-trunks. Where are there trees? In the wood . . . And so he went all the long hot way back to the edge of the wood, and got a pair of slender fir saplings for himself (there are no tree-spirits in the fir).

Moomintroll and the Snork maiden hunted together. They talked about Moomin Valley and the cave, and soon completely forgot what they were hunting for.

'My pappa has built a wonderful bridge,' said Moomintroll, for about the third time, 'but mostly he writes in a book called "Memoirs". It's all about what he has done in his life, and as soon as he does something else he writes that down too.'

'Then surely he hasn't got time to do very much?' said the Snork maiden.

'Oh, well,' said Moomintroll. 'He makes sure of doing things now and again, even if it's only to give himself something to write about.'

'Tell me about that terrible flood you had,' said the Snork maiden.

'Oh yes, it was dreadful!' said Moomintroll. 'The water just rose and rose, until in the end mamma and Sniff and I were standing on a little mound with hardly room even for our tails.'

'Phew!' said the Snork maiden. 'How high was the water?'

'Five times higher than I am, or perhaps more,' said Moomintroll. 'About as high as that pole over there.'

'Fancy!' exclaimed the Snork maiden. And they wandered on thinking about the flood.

After a while Moomintroll stopped and asked: 'Didn't I say "as high as that *pole* over there"?'

'Yes. Why?' asked the Snork maiden.

'Because I've just remembered we're looking for poles,' Moomintroll answered. 'We must go back and fetch it.'

They trudged back along the beach till they found the pole again. It was very long and painted red and white.

'It's one of those posts they use at sea to mark rocks from one side,' said Moomintroll, 'and there's the one for the other side.'

They were in what had been a little bay before the sea had dried up, and the beach was littered with wreckage, piles of driftwood, birch-bark and seaweed. The Snork maiden

found the knob off the top of a ship's mast, but it was too big to take with them. Instead she picked up a bottle with a gilded stopper which had drifted all the way from Mexico. And soon afterwards they came across a very long plank which, broken in two, would do very well for the second pair of stilts.

They set off back very pleased with themselves, and found the others already practising. Snufkin was demonstrating proudly on a fishing-rod and a hop-pole, and

Sniff was trying to keep his balance on a broom-stick and the pole that still had their flag on the end of it.

'You ought to have seen me a minute ago,' he cried, and immediately fell smack on his nose.

'You have to do it like this,' said the Snork, climbing over a sandbank. 'It's like wearing seven-league boots!'

The Snork maiden whimpered with fright when they hoisted her up on her stilts. But after a time she was better than any of them, strutting about with such an air that you'd have thought she had worn them all her life.

'I think that's pretty good now,' said Snufkin, when they had been balancing and staggering and falling for an hour or so. 'Let's start.'

One after another, with their stilts under their arms, they began to climb down the difficult slippery path to the abyss.

It was very depressing down there on the sea bottom. The seaweed, which looks so beautiful waving in green transparent water, was all flat and black, and the fish floundered pathetically in half-dried-up pools.

The steam was like a smoke-screen above them, and through it the comet shone with a dim eerie light.

'It's almost the same as the land of the hot springs,' said Snufkin.

'It smells awful,' said Sniff, wrinkling his nose. 'Don't forget I'm not to blame for this – I warned you . . .'

'How goes it?' cried Moomintroll to the Snork maiden through the steam.

'Fine, thanks!' came a faint answering cry.

And on they stalked like long-legged insects, across the bottom of the sea, while the ground sloped gradually down. Here and there great dark green mountains rose; their tops had once been little islands where people had landed and children enjoyed themselves splashing about in the water.

'Never again will I swim in deep water,' said Sniff with a shiver. 'Just to think that all this was underneath!' He squinted down a dark cleft where there was still some water left, and no doubt a strange swarming underwater life.

'But it's beautiful although it's so awful,' said Snufkin. 'And nobody has ever been here before us! What's that over there?'

'A treasure chest!' screamed Sniff. 'Oh! Let's go and see!'

'We can't take it with us anyhow,' said the Snork. 'Let it be. I expect we shall find even more extraordinary things before we get through this place.'

Now they were moving between jagged black rocks, and had to go very carefully for fear of the stilts getting caught. Suddenly in the gloom in front of them a great dark shape loomed up.

'What's that?' gasped Moomintroll, stopping so suddenly that he nearly fell on his nose.

'Perhaps it's something that bites!' said Sniff, anxiously.

Slowly they advanced and peeped at the shape from behind a rock.

'A ship!' exclaimed the Snork. 'A shipwreck!'

How miserable she looked, poor ship! Her mast was broken, and barnacles covered her rotted hull. Her sails and rigging had long ago been swept away by the current, and her golden figurehead was cracked and discoloured.

'Do you think there's anybody on board?' whispered the Snork maiden.

'I expect they were rescued by lifeboat,' said Moomintroll. 'Come away! This is horrible.'

'Wait a minute,' said Sniff, hopping down from his stilts, 'I can see something gold – something shining . . .'

'Remember what happened with the garnets and the

giant lizard!' called Snufkin. 'Much better let it be!'

But Sniff bent down and pulled a dagger with a golden hilt out of the sand. It was set with opals that shone like moonlight and the blade gleamed coldly. Sniff lifted up his find and shouted with excitement.

'Oh, so beautiful!' exclaimed the Snork maiden and completely lost her balance. She rocked backwards and forwards, and suddenly shot right over the side of the ship, and disappeared into the hold. Moomintroll let out one shriek and dashed to her rescue.

His rush was slightly held up by the slipperiness of the deck, but he was soon peering down into the dark hold.

'Are you there?' he cried anxiously.

'Yes, I'm here,' piped the Snork maiden.

'Are you all right?' asked Moomintroll, jumping down to her, and finding with a shock that the water came up to his middle, and that it had a horrible stagnant smell.

'I'm all right,' said the Snork maiden, 'only so frightened.'

'Sniff is an absolute pest,' said Moomintroll furiously. 'Always wanting to run after everything that shines or glitters.'

'Well, I do understand him,' said the Snork maiden. 'Ornaments are such fun, especially if they are made of gold and jewels. Don't you think we might find some more treasure in here . . . ?'

'It's so dark,' said Moomintroll, 'and there may be dangerous animals about.'

'Yes, I suppose you're right,' said the Snork maiden obediently. 'Be a kind Moomintroll then and help me out of here.'

So Moomintroll lifted her up onto the edge of the hatchway.

The Snork maiden immediately took out her looking-glass to see if it was broken, but, thank goodness, the glass was whole and all the rubies were still on the back. But as she was titivating herself, a horrifying picture came into the looking-glass. There was the dark hold, and there was Moomintroll who was just climbing out – but behind in a dark corner there was something else. Something that moved. Something that crept slowly nearer to Moomintroll.

The Snork maiden threw down the looking-glass and yelled with all her might: 'Look out! There's something behind you!'

Moomintroll looked over his shoulder, and what he saw was a huge octopus, the most dangerous of deep-sea creatures, squirming slowly out of a corner towards him. He tried desperately to clamber up and reach the Snork maiden's paw, but he slid back on the slimy planks and

splashed into the water again. By this time Snufkin and the
others had come up on the deck to see what was happening,
and they tried to poke the octopus with their stilts, but it
didn't have the slightest effect on him: he just crept relent-
lessly nearer to Moomintroll, his long tentacles already
groping after his prey.

Then the Snork maiden had an idea. She had often
played with a looking-glass in the sun, making its reflection
shine into her brother's eyes to dazzle him. So now she
picked up her ruby looking-glass and tried the same thing
against the octopus, only shining the comet instead of the
sun into his eyes. It was most successful. The octopus
stopped at once, and while he was dazzled and didn't know
what to do, Moomintroll clambered up by his stilts and was
hauled on deck by the others.

They left that dreadful ship without wasting any time, and hardly drew breath before they were several sea-miles away from it.

Then Moomintroll said to the Snork maiden: 'You saved my life you know! And in such a clever way too! I shall ask Snufkin to write a poem in your honour, because I'm afraid I can't write poetry myself.'

The Snork maiden lowered her eyes and began to change colour with pleasure.

'I was very happy to do it,' she whispered. 'I would save your life eight times a day if only I could.'

'And I wouldn't mind eight octopuses attacking me every day if I could only be saved from them by you,' said Moomintroll gallantly.

'If you've quite finished babbling to each other,' said Sniff, 'perhaps we could go on.'

The sand had got more even now, and there were huge shells, with horns and spirals, in the most wonderful colours, such as purple, midnight-blue, and sea-green, strewn about all over the place.

The Snork maiden wanted to stay and admire every one, and listen to the call of the sea which lay hidden inside them, but the Snork hurried her on.

Enormous crabs were sidling in and out between the shells, telling each other how strange it was that the water had disappeared. They wondered who had taken it away and when it would come back. 'Thank goodness I'm not a jelly-fish!' said one. 'Out of the water they are nothing but miserable little splodges, but *we* of course are equally happy wherever we are.'

'I feel so sorry for anybody who wasn't born a crab,' said another. 'It's quite possible that this drying-up of the sea has been arranged especially so that we shall have more space to live in.'

'What an excellent thought! Why not a world peopled entirely by crabs?' exclaimed a third, waving his claws.

'Self-satisfied creatures!' muttered Snufkin. 'Try dazzling *them* with the looking-glass, and see if they know what to do then.'

The Snork maiden fixed the comet's reflection again, and shone it in the crabs' eyes. There was a terrible upheaval. Chattering with fright, the crabs rushed wildly in all directions, knocking each other over on the way, and buried their heads in pools of water.

Moomintroll and the others had a good laugh and went on their way, and after a while Snufkin thought he would play a tune. But not a sound could he get out of his mouth-organ; the steam had rusted it up.

'Oh dear!' he said sadly, 'this is about the worst thing that could happen.'

'Pappa will mend it for you when we get home,' said Moomintroll. 'He can mend anything, if only he gets around to it.'

All about them stretched the strange sea landscape, which had been covered by millions of tons of water since the beginning of the world.

'You know it's rather solemn to be down here,' said the Snork. 'We must be pretty near the deepest part of the ocean by now.'

But when they reached the biggest chasm of all they didn't dare go down. The sides sloped steeply and the bottom was obscured in green gloom. Perhaps there *was* no bottom! Perhaps the biggest octopuses in the world lived down there, brooding in the slime; creatures that nobody had ever seen, far less imagined. But the Snork maiden gazed longingly at an enormous and beautiful shell that was poised on the very brink of the chasm. It was a lovely pale colour, only to be found in the depths of the sea where no light penetrates, and its dusky heart glowed temptingly. The shell sang softly to herself the age-old song of the sea.

'Oh!' sighed the Snork maiden. 'I should like to live in that shell. I want to go inside and see who is whispering in there.'

'It's only the sea,' said Moomintroll. 'Every wave that dies on the beach sings a little song to a shell. But you mustn't go inside because it's a labyrinth and you may never come out again.'

So she was at last persuaded to go on, and they started to hurry, as dusk was falling, and they had not found anywhere to sleep. They could only see soft outlines of each other through the damp sea mist, and it was uncannily silent. There were none of the small sounds that liven up the evening on land: the pattering of small animal feet, leaves moving in the night breeze, the cry of a bird, of a stone dislodged by somebody's foot.

A fire would never draw on that damp ground, and they dared not sleep amongst the unknown dangers that might be lurking about, so in the end they decided to pitch camp on a high pointed rock, which they could just reach by their stilts. They had to keep watch, so Moomintroll took the first and decided to take the Snork maiden's too, and while the others curled up tightly together and slept, he sat staring out over the desolate sea bottom. It was lit by the red glow of the comet, and shadows like black velvet lay across the sand.

Moomintroll thought how frightened the earth must be feeling with that great ball of fire coming nearer and nearer to her. Then he thought about how much he loved everything; the forest and the sea, the rain and the wind, the sunshine, the grass and the moss, and how impossible it would be to live without them all, and this made him feel very, very sad. But after a while he stopped worrying.

'Mamma will know what to do,' he said to himself.

CHAPTER 10

*Which is about a Hemulen's stamp-collection, a swarm of
grass-hoppers and a horrible tornado.*

WHEN Sniff woke up next day the first thing he said was:
'*It's* coming tomorrow!'

'It's so big!' said the Snork maiden. 'Nearly as big as a
house.'

All the steam had disappeared in the heat of the comet,
and they could see right across to the other side where the
bottom of the sea gradually sloped up to the beach again.
They hadn't far to go.

'Trees!' shouted Snufkin, pointing, and they all set off
in a tremendous hurry to get there, without even waiting to
put their stilts on.

'Silver poplars!' puffed Moomintroll as he stumped up
the sandy beach. 'Moomin Valley can't be far off now.'

The Snork began to whistle, and they were all so pleased
to be on dry land again that they hugged each other in their
excitement.

Then they set off again for home.

As they were going along they met a house-troll coming towards them on a bicycle. He was red in the face with heat (for house-trolls can never take off their fur coats). On the carrier he had two or three suitcases, and packages and parcels of all kinds dangled from the handlebars. On his back sat a baby house-troll in a bag.

'Are you leaving?' shouted Sniff.

The house-troll climbed off his bicycle and said: 'You may well ask, little animal. Everybody who lives in the neighbourhood of Moomin Valley is leaving. I don't think there's a single person who intends to stay there and wait for the comet.'

'How is it you all think the comet is going to fall just there?' asked the Snork.

'Well, you might say, by word of beak,' said the house-troll. 'The Muskrat sent the information round through the birds, and it is quite obvious to any self-respecting house-troll that the comet will fall in Moomin Valley.'

'Oh, by the way,' said Moomintroll. 'I believe our families are distantly related, and when I left home my mother told me to give you her kind regards if we happened to meet.'

'Thank you, thank you,' said the house-troll hurriedly. 'And the same to your poor mother. It may be the last time I shall be able to send greetings to her, because she and your father absolutely refuse to leave the valley. They said they had to wait until you and Sniff got back!'

'Then we had better hurry,' said Moomintroll in a worried voice. 'If you go past a post office will you please send a telegram home saying that we are on the way and coming as fast as we can? Make it a greetings telegram please!'

'Yes, I'll do that,' said the house-troll climbing on to his bicycle. 'Well, goodbye, and may the Protector-of-all-House-and-Moomintrolls watch over you!' And he peddled earnestly away.

'Did you ever see so much luggage!' said Snufkin. 'And the poor chap was quite exhausted. Oh, isn't it wonderful not to own anything!' And he threw his old green hat up gaily in the air.

'I don't know about that,' said Sniff, gazing lovingly at his little jewelled dagger. 'It's nice to have beautiful things that really belong to you.'

'Now we must get on,' said Moomintroll. 'They're waiting for us at home, and I'm sure that can't be much fun.'

On the way they met crowds of fleeing creatures; some walking, some driving, some riding, and some even taking their houses with them on wheelbarrows. They all kept glancing fearfully at the sky and hardly anyone had time to stop and talk.

'It's strange,' said Moomintroll, 'but it seems to me that we aren't as afraid as any of these people, although we're going to the most dangerous place of all, and they're leaving it.'

'That's because we are so extremely brave,' said Sniff.

'H'm,' said Moomintroll. 'I think,' he mused, 'it must be because we've sort of got to know the comet. We were the first ones to find out that it was coming. We've seen it grow from a tiny dot to a great sun . . . How lonely it must be up there, with everybody afraid of it!'

The Snork maiden put her paw into Moomintroll's. 'Anyway,' she said, 'if you're not afraid, I'm not either!'

Soon they stopped by the wayside to have lunch, and there sat a Hemulen with a stamp album on his lap.

'All this fuss and rush!' he was muttering to himself. 'Crowds of people everywhere, and not one of them can tell me just what it's all about.'

'Good morning,' said Moomintroll. 'I suppose you aren't by any chance a relation of the Hemulen we met in the Lonely Mountains? He collected butterflies.'

'That must have been my cousin on my father's side,' answered the Hemulen. 'He is very stupid. We don't even know each other now. I broke off our relationship.'

'Why was that?' asked Sniff.

'He had no interest in anything but his old butterflies,' said the Hemulen. 'The earth could crack under his feet and it wouldn't bother him.'

'That's exactly what's going to happen now,' said the Snork. 'To be precise, at 8.42 tomorrow evening.'

'What?' said the Hemulen. 'Well, as I said, there has

been a tremendous fuss going on here. I had been sorting my stamps for a whole week and all my perforations, watermarks and so on were in different piles, when what happens? Somebody goes off with the table I am working on. Somebody else snatches the chair from under me. Then the very house disappears. And here I sit with my stamps in a complete muddle, and nobody has bothered to tell me what it's all about.'

'Listen now, Hemul,' said Snufkin slowly and clearly. 'It's about a comet that is going to collide with the earth tomorrow.'

'Collide?' said the Hemulen. 'Has that anything to do with stamp-collecting?'

'No, it hasn't,' said Snufkin. 'It has to do with a comet – a wild star with a tail. And if it comes here there won't be much of your stamp-collection left.'

'Heaven protect me!' gasped the Hemulen, and with this somewhat illogical request he gathered up his dress (a hemulen always wears a dress – nobody knows why – perhaps they have never thought of trousers), and asked what he should do next.

'Come with us,' said the Snork maiden. 'We've found a cave where both you and your stamp-collection can hide.'

And that was how the Hemulen joined the party returning to Moomin Valley. Once they had to go back several miles to look for a rare stamp that had fluttered out of his album, and once he had a quarrel with the Snork (who insisted that it was a 'dispute' though anybody could *see* that it was a quarrel) about something that somebody had forgotten to do. But on the whole they got on quite well with the Hemulen.

They had left the country road long ago and reached a

great wood of silver poplars and oaks with a few plum trees dotted about, when Sniff stopped and listened.

'Can you hear anything?' he asked.

Very, very faintly they heard a whirring, buzzing sound. It came nearer and nearer until they were deafened by the roar. The Snork maiden held Moomintroll's paw very tight.

'Look!' screamed Sniff.

Suddenly the red sky was darkened by a cloud of flying creatures that first sank, and then dived straight into the wood.

'It's a swarm of grass-hoppers!' cried the Snork. They all hid behind a stone and looked cautiously out at the wild green bandits that swarmed in their millions amongst the branches.

'Have the grass-hoppers gone mad?' whispered the Snork maiden.

'We – will – eat!' chanted the nearest grass-hopper.

'We – are – eating!' sang another. 'We – are – eating!' chorused all the other grass-hoppers who were gnawing, tearing and biting at everything in sight.

'It makes me hungry to look at them,' said the Hemulen. 'This is even worse than the last fuss. I do hope they don't eat stamp-albums.'

'Can any of you see that grass-hopper musician who was drinking beer at the dance?' asked Snufkin.

'He was the tame, meadow sort,' answered the Snork. 'These are wild Egyptian grass-hoppers.'

It was quite fascinating to see how fast they ate. In a short while the poor trees were naked. Not a leaf was left – not even a blade of grass.

Moomintroll sighed. 'I have heard that grass-hoppers always ravage the country before any great catastrophe,' he said.

'What's a catastrophe?' asked Sniff.

'It's something as bad as it can possibly be,' said Moomintroll. 'Like earthquakes, and tidal waves, and volcanoes. And tornadoes. And plagues.'

'In other words – "fuss",' said the Hemulen. 'One never has any peace.'

'What was it like in Egypt?' squeaked Sniff to the nearest grass-hopper.

'Oh, short rations you know,' he sang. 'But look out, little friends, beware of the great wind!'

'We – have – eaten!' sang all the grass-hoppers, and with a burst of chirping and croaking the whole swarm rose from the bare skeleton of the wood.

'What dreadful creatures!' exclaimed Snufkin, and the little procession trudged dejectedly on through the silent desolation that the grass-hoppers had made.

'I'm thirsty!' wailed the Snork maiden. 'Aren't we

nearly there yet? Snufkin, do play the Higgely-piggely song. It's just how I feel now.'

'The mouth-organ is broken,' protested Snufkin. 'There are only a couple of notes that will play at all.'

'Then let's have it with them,' said the Snork maiden, and Snufkin played:

> Higg – –, pig – –,
> Path – – wigg – –,
> – – – four.
> Almost – –
> On little – –;
> – – – door.

'I didn't think much of that,' said the Hemulen. And they plodded on, their feet more tired than ever.

Meanwhile far off in Egypt a tornado had been born, and now it was flying on black wings across the desert, whistling ominously as it went, whirling up sticks and straws, and growing blacker and stronger every minute. It began sweeping trees away and lifting the roofs from the houses in its path. Then it threw itself across the sea and, climbing over the mountains, came at last to the place where the Valley of the Moomins lay.

Sniff, who had long ears, heard it first. 'It must be another swarm of grass-hoppers,' he said.

They all raised their noses and listened.

'It's the storm this time,' said the Snork maiden. And she was right. It was the great storm the grass-hopper had warned them about.

The heralds of the tornado came howling through the bare tree trunks. They tore off Moomintroll's medal and blew it right into the top of a fir tree, they bowled Sniff over four times and tried to take Snufkin's hat away from him. The Hemulen clutched his stamp album, cursing and

muttering, and the whole lot of them were blown through the wood and out on to an open moor.

'This ought to be arranged a little better,' shouted the Snork. 'A fine wind like this and nothing to sail with!'

'Nothing to sail *in* either,' said Snufkin, 'which is more important.'

They crept down under the roots of a tree to discuss things.

'I made a glider when I was small,' said Moomintroll. 'It flew very well . . .'

'A balloon wouldn't be such a bad idea,' said the Snork maiden. 'I had a sausage one once. Yellow.'

Just then a baby tornado dived under the tree roots and took hold of the Hemulen's stamp album, whirling it high up in the air. With a howl of anguish he leapt to his feet and set off after his treasure. He staggered and fluttered, and the wind got under his wide skirt and carried him off over the heather. He flapped away like a great kite.

The Snork looked thoughtfully after him and said: 'I think I've got an idea. Follow me all of you.'

They found the Hemulen some distance away, sitting and moaning to himself quite overcome with despair.

'Hemul,' said the Snork. 'This is all a terrible catastrophe, but will you be kind enough to lend us your dress for a short time. We want to make a balloon out of it.'

'Oh! My stamp collection!' wailed the Hemulen. 'My life's work, my magnificent collection! Rare, unique, irreplaceable! The best in the world!'

'Listen, take off your dress for a minute will you?' said the Snork.

'What?' said the Hemulen. 'Take off my *dress*?'

'Yes,' they all shouted. 'We want to make a balloon out of it.'

The Hemulen went red with anger. 'Here I sit in distress,' he said, 'after a terrible accident caused only by your rotten old catastrophe. And now you want to take my dress!'

'Listen,' said the Snork. 'We'll save your stamp album if you'll only do what we say. But hurry up! This is only the beginning of the tornado – like a gale warning. When the real thing comes it's safest to be up in the air.'

'I don't care a straw about your tornado *or* your comet,' shouted the Hemulen who had worked himself up into a real rage. 'When it concerns my stamps . . .'

But he got no farther, for they all threw themselves on top of him and in a twinkling they had pulled his dress over his head. It was a very large dress with a frill round the bottom, which he had inherited from his aunt. They only had to tie up the neck and the armholes and it made a perfect balloon.

The Hemulen cursed and muttered fiercely, but nobody paid any attention to him, because away on the horizon they could see the real tornado approaching. It looked like a great spiral-shaped cloud, and it came whirling over the forest with a wild howling roar, rooting up the trees and throwing them down like match-sticks.

'Hold on with all your might,' shouted Moomintroll, and they all caught hold of the frill on the Hemulen's dress, and knotted their tails together for safety's sake. The tornado had arrived!

For quite a long time they could neither hear nor see. But the Hemulen's dress lifted them up, higher and higher, and carried them over the moor, over mountain tops and dried up lakes, on and on, and twilight came, and then darkness, before the tornado lost its breath and died. At last they came to rest and found the balloon had hitched itself up in a tall plum tree.

'Well, strike me pink!' exclaimed Moomintroll. 'Are you all still here?'

'I'm here,' said the Hemulen, 'and I wish to point out now, before anything else happens, that I will not join in these childish games in future. If you *will* fool about like this you must do it without me.'

This time they all felt too exhausted to start explaining everything to the Hemulen again.

'I'm still here, and I've got my looking-glass too,' said the Snork maiden.

'And I've got my hat,' said Snufkin, 'and the mouth-organ.'

'But my exercise book might be *anywhere*,' said the Snork miserably, 'and I had written down everything that has to be done when a comet comes. *Now* what are we going to do?'

'Well never mind that now,' said Moomintroll. 'Where's Sniff?'

'Here,' piped a feeble voice, 'if it really *is* me and not some poor bit of wreckage left over by the storm.'

'It's you all right,' said the Hemulen. 'I'd know your squeak anywhere. And perhaps I could have my dress back now.'

'Why, certainly,' said Moomintroll. 'And thank you for the loan of it.'

The Hemulen grumbled and puffed as he pulled his dress over his head, but luckily he couldn't see in the dark how the tornado had treated it!

They spent the night in the plum tree, very close together, and they were so tired after their journey that they didn't wake up till twelve o'clock the next day.

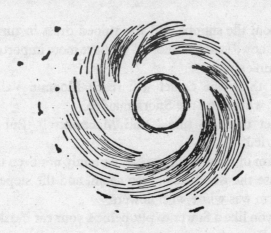

CHAPTER II

Which is about a coffee-party, the flight to the cave and the arrival of the comet.

THE seventh of October was windless and very hot. Moomintroll woke up and gave a huge yawn. Then he shut his mouth with a snap and his eyes opened very wide.

'Do you realize what today is?' he asked.

'The comet!' whispered Sniff.

My goodness, it was big! The red had turned to yellowish-white now, and round it was a circle of dancing flames. The wood seemed to be waiting, breathless . . . The ants were in their ant hills, the birds in their nests, and every one of the little creeping things of the forest, who had not already left the place, had found somewhere to hide.

'What's the time?' asked Moomintroll.

'Ten past twelve,' answered the Snork.

Nobody said another word. They clambered down the tree and set off as fast as they could towards home.

Only the Hemulen went on making small, angry noises to

himself, about the stamps and the ruined dress in turns.

'Be quiet now,' said the Snork. 'We have more important things to think about.'

'Do you think the comet will reach Moomin Valley before us?' whispered the Snork maiden.

'We'll get there in time,' said Moomintroll. But he looked worried.

The swarm of grass-hoppers had certainly not been this way, because the wood was green again, and the slope in front of them was white with flowers.

'Would you like a flower to put behind your ear?' asked Moomintroll.

'Good gracious, no!' answered the Snork maiden. 'I'm much too worried to think about things like that.'

Meanwhile Sniff had gone ahead, and suddenly they heard him give a shout of excitement.

'Some new fuss I suppose,' said the Hemulen.

'Hi! Hullo! Hurry up!' shrieked Sniff. 'Run! Come on!' And he put his paws in his mouth and gave a piercing whistle.

They set off at a run through the trees, Moomintroll in

front. As he ran he sniffed, and a delicious smell of baking bread floated up to him. The trees thinned out – and Moomintroll stopped suddenly with a shout of surprise and happiness.

There below him lay the Valley of the Moomins. And in the middle amongst the plum and poplar trees, stood a blue Moominhouse, as blue and peaceful and wonderful as when

he had left it. And inside his mother was peacefully baking bread and cakes.

'*Now* everything is going to be all right,' said Moomintroll happily, and he was so overcome that he had to sit down.

'There's the bridge!' said the Snork maiden, 'and there's the poplar tree you talked about that is so good to climb. What a beautiful house it is!'

Moominmamma was in the kitchen decorating a big cake with pale yellow lemon peel and slices of crystalized pear. The words 'To my darling Moomintroll' were written round it in chocolate, and on the top there was a glittering star of spun sugar.

Moominmamma was whistling softly to herself, and now and then she looked out of the window.

Moominpappa was wandering nervously from room to room getting thoroughly in the way. 'They should be here soon,' he said, 'it's half-past one.'

'They'll be here all right,' said Moominmamma confidently. 'Wait a moment while I take away the cake! Sniff shall have the basin to lick out – he always has it.'

'If he comes,' said Moominpappa, and sighed deeply.

At that moment the Muskrat came and sat down in a corner.

'Well, what about the comet?' asked Moominmamma.

'It's coming nearer,' said the Muskrat. 'This is a time for weeping and wailing, sure enough. But of course that sort of thing doesn't affect a philosopher like me.'

'Well, I hope you'll take good care of your whiskers when the time comes,' said Moominmamma kindly. 'It would be a pity to get them singed. Will you have a ginger-nut?'

'Well, thank you – perhaps a small one,' said the Muskrat. When he had eaten eight ginger-nuts he said: 'Young Moomintroll seems to be coming down the hill, accompanied by the strangest looking party. I don't know if that interests you at all.'

'*Moomintroll?*' screamed Moominmamma. 'Why didn't you say so before?' And she rushed out, closely followed by Moominpappa.

There they were, running across the bridge! First Moomintroll and Sniff, then Snufkin, then the Snorks, and last of all the Hemulen, who had not got over his bad temper.

They all fell into each other's arms and Moominmamma burst out: 'My darling Moomin-child, I thought I should never see you again!'

'You should have seen me fighting with the poisonous bush!' said Moomintroll. 'Snip! Off came one arm! Snap! Off came another, and in the end there was only a stump left!'

'Well!' said Moominmamma. 'And who is this little girl?'

'It's the Snork maiden,' said Moomintroll, bringing her forward. 'She was the one I rescued from the poisonous bush. And this is Snufkin who is one of the world's wanderers. This is the Hemulen; the expert philatterist!'

'Oh!' said Moominpappa, 'really?' And then it dawned on him. 'Why, yes,' he said, 'I remember collecting stamps in my youth. A very interesting hobby.'

'It isn't my hobby – it's my work,' retorted the Hemulen rudely. (He had slept badly.)

'In that case,' said Moominpappa, 'perhaps you could give me your opinion of a stamp album that was blown here yesterday evening by the tornado.'

'Stamp album, did you say?' exclaimed the Hemulen, 'that blew here?'

'Why, yes,' put in Moominmamma. 'I made the dough for the bread last night, and this morning it was full of little bits of sticky paper.'

'Sticky paper!' screeched the Hemulen. 'Those must be my rarest of rare specimens. Are they still there? Where are they? Surely in the name of all Hemulens you haven't thrown them away?'

'They're all hanging up to dry,' said Moominmamma, pointing to a washing line under the plum trees.

The Hemulen rushed off.

'Now there's some life in him,' said Sniff laughing. 'But he wouldn't run two steps if the comet were after him.'

'Yes, the comet,' said Moominmamma anxiously. 'The Muskrat says that it will fall in my kitchen garden this evening. It's most annoying because I've just weeded it.'

'I suggest that we hold a meeting about it in Moominhouse,' said the Snork. 'I mean – if you don't mind of course.'

'No, no, of course not,' said Moominpappa. 'Come along in. Make yourselves at home!'

'There are some fresh ginger-nuts,' said Moominmamma, slightly flurried, putting out the new coffee cups with roses and lilies on them. '*What* a good thing you came home in time dears!'

'Did you get the telegram that the house-troll sent?' asked Sniff.

'Yes,' said Moominpappa, 'but the letters were all topsy-turvy, and most of it was just exclamation marks. The house-troll was obviously too nervous to send off any telegrams.'

Just then Moominmamma leaned out of the window and

cried 'Coffee!' and they all trooped inside, except the Hemulen. He was busy spreading out all his stamps and sorting them into different piles, and he only muttered crossly that he hadn't time.

'Well,' said the Snork, 'now we can come to the point. Unfortunately I have lost the exercise book where I had written down exactly what to do about escaping from comets, but one thing stands out as clear as the nose on my face, and that is that we must find a sheltered place to hide in.'

'You make such a fuss about it all,' said his sister. 'It's quite simple. All we have to do is to creep into Moomintroll's cave and take our most precious belongings with us!'

'And lots of food,' said Sniff. 'And it's *my* cave, by-the-way!'

'Good gracious me!' exclaimed Moominmamma. 'Have you got a cave all of your own?'

This set Moomintroll and Sniff off on a long description of how they had found the cave, what a wonderful cave it was, and how it was an absolutely perfect hiding place. They both talked at the same time, each trying to speak louder than the other, and the result was that Sniff upset his coffee cup on the table cloth.

'Really!' exclaimed Moominmamma in exasperation. 'It's obvious that you've all been living like hooligans while you've been away. Sniff, you had better eat on the mat. And the cake basin is in the sink – you can take it with you if you like.'

Sniff dived under the table covered with confusion, and the meeting continued.

'I've always believed in letting everybody do his bit,' said the Snork pompously. 'We must all carry our things up to the cave as soon as possible, because it's three o'clock already. Perhaps my sister and I could carry the bed-clothes?'

'That will be fine,' said Moominmamma. 'I'll take the jam. Sniff dear, will you start emptying the drawers of the bureau, because all those things must be packed.'

So began the biggest running and carrying and packing you ever saw. Moominpappa filled the wheelbarrow, and Moominmamma bustled about looking for string and news-paper. (It was like being evacuated to the country in war-time with only a few hours' notice.)

Over and over again Moominpappa pushed the wheel-barrow through the wood to the beach and unloaded it on the sand. Then Moomintroll and Snufkin hoisted every-thing up to the cave on a rope.

Meanwhile the others were collecting all that it was possible to move in the house, down to the door-handles of the cupboards and the cords of the blinds.

'I don't intend to leave a single thing for that old comet,' muttered Moominmamma, pulling the bath-tub through the door. 'Snork, dear, do run and pull the radishes in the kitchen garden, and Sniff, you can carry the cake up to the cave, but be very careful with it!'

Moominpappa came puffing up with the wheelbarrow. 'Hurry up, all of you!' he said. 'It will soon be getting dark, and the hole in the roof of the cave still has to be blocked up.'

'Yes, yes,' said Moominmamma. 'Coming directly. I just want the shells round my rhubarb bed. And the best of the roses.'

'No,' said Moominpappa decidedly, 'we'll leave *those* behind anyway. Now get into the bath my dear, and I'll wheel you up to the cave. Where is the Hemulen?'

'He's counting his stamps,' said the Snork maiden. 'Nothing else seems to interest him.'

'Hullo! Hemul!' shouted the Snork. 'Hurry up for goodness sake. The comet will be here in a minute and then your stamps will most certainly be lost.'

'Oh, heaven preserve me!' exclaimed the Hemulen, and hopped straight into the bath-tub, where he sat firmly with his stamp album, refusing to budge.

Then the whole party set off on the last journey up to the cave. It was gloomy and desolate on the shore, with the great gap that had been the sea in front of them, the dark red sky overhead, and behind, the forest panting in the heat. The comet was very near now. It glowed white hot and looked enormous as it rushed towards Moomin Valley.

'Where's the Muskrat?' Moominmamma suddenly asked in a horrified voice.

'He wouldn't come,' answered Moominpappa. 'He said it was unnecessary and undignified for a philosopher to rush about like this. I had to leave him, but I let him keep the hammock.'

'Oh, well,' sighed Moominmamma. 'It's difficult to understand philosophers. Out of the way now children, pappa is going to hoist up the bath.'

Moomintroll, Sniff and Snufkin heaved and shouted up in the cave, while Moominpappa and the Snorks pushed and gave orders from the sand, and the bath wobbled up and down, slipped and was heaved up again, until at last it was on the ledge outside the cave.

Moominmamma had been sitting on the sand all this time mopping her forehead, and now she gave a great sigh and exclaimed: 'What a move!'

The Hemulen, of course, had taken no part in the removal of the bath apart from sitting in it. He had already crept into the cave and was arranging his stamps. 'Always some fuss and hurry,' he muttered, 'if only I could make out what's come over them all.'

And while it got hotter and hotter and darker and darker the hands of the clock slowly crept nearer to seven.

They couldn't get the bath through the opening of the cave, and the Snork wanted to hold a meeting about it, but as there wasn't time for that they decided to hoist it right up to the roof to stop up the opening there.

Moominmamma made beds for them all on the soft sandy

floor of the cave and lit the lamp, while Snufkin hung a blanket up in front of the door.

'Do you think that will be enough protection?' asked Moomintroll.

Snufkin pulled a bottle out of his pocket and waved it triumphantly. 'Have you forgotten the underground sun-oil I got from the fire-spirit?' he asked. 'The last drop is just enough to paint the outside of the blanket, and then twenty comets won't be able to burn it up!'

'It won't stain the blanket I hope?' asked Moomin-mamma anxiously.

Just then they heard a sniffing and rustling outside the cave, and a nose poked under the blanket, then came two black eyes and then a whole Muskrat.

'Oh!' exclaimed Sniff. 'You came after all Uncle Muskrat?'

'Yes, I found it difficult to think down there in that heat,' said the Muskrat, lumbering off to a corner with great dignity.

'Now we're ready,' said Moominpappa. 'What's the time?'

'Twenty-five past seven,' said the Snork.

'Then we've got time to taste the cake,' said Moominmamma. 'Sniff, where did you put it?'

'Somewhere over there,' said Sniff, pointing to the corner where the Muskrat was sitting.

'Where?' asked Moominmamma. 'I can't see it. Muskrat, have you seen a cake anywhere?'

'I don't bother myself over things like cakes,' said the Muskrat, twisting his moustache solemnly. 'I don't see them, taste them or feel them in any way, ever.'

'Yes, but where in the world has that cake got to?' said Moominmamma in despair. 'Sniff, you can't have eaten it all on the way?'

'It was too big,' said Sniff innocently.

'So you ate some of it!' screamed Moomintroll. 'Come on, own up!'

'Only the star on the top,' said Sniff, 'and that was rather hard.' He crawled under the mattress and hid himself.

'Miserable children,' said Moominmamma, sitting down on a chair and suddenly feeling rather tired.

The Snork maiden looked sharply at the Muskrat. 'Would you mind moving a moment, Uncle Muskrat?' she asked.

'Here I sit and here I stay,' said the Muskrat.

'There you sit on our cake,' said the Snork maiden.

Then the Muskrat got up, and oh dear, you never saw such a mess as there was on his bottom. And as for the cake . . .

'That was unnecessary anyhow!' piped Sniff.

'My cake too,' groaned Moomintroll. 'In my honour!'

'Now I shall be sticky for the rest of my life I suppose,' said the Muskrat bitterly. 'I only hope I can bear it like a man and a philosopher.'

'Be quiet all of you,' cried Moominmamma. 'It's still the same cake – just a different shape that's all. Now bring up your plates and we'll share it out all the same.' And she

cut the squashed cake into nine equal pieces and doled it out. Then she filled a basin with warm water and told the Muskrat to sit down in it.

'This has completely disturbed my peace,' he complained. 'A philosopher should be protected against the rude happenings of everyday life.'

'Never mind,' said Moominmamma, consolingly. 'You'll soon feel better.'

'But I *do* mind,' said the Muskrat peevishly. 'Never any peace . . .' And he mumbled on.

It grew hotter and hotter in the cave. They all sat in separate corners, and waited. Now and again there was a sigh or somebody passed an obvious remark. Otherwise there was silence.

Suddenly Moomintroll jumped up.

'We've forgotten the silk-monkey!' he cried.

'So we have,' said Moominmamma. 'What a dreadful thing! I saw her only yesterday chasing crabs.'

'She must be rescued,' said Moomintroll decidedly. 'Does anybody know where she lives?'

'She doesn't live anywhere,' said Moominpappa. 'I'm afraid she must be left to her fate. We haven't got time to look for her.'

'Oh, please don't go, dear Moomintroll!' entreated the Snork maiden.

'I must,' he answered. 'I'll be back. And don't worry!'

'Take my watch so that you can keep an eye on the time,' said the Snork. 'And be as quick as you can. It's a quarter past eight already.'

'Then I've got twenty-seven minutes,' said Moomintroll. He hugged his anxious mamma, swallowed the last bit of cake, and dived under the blanket.

It was like walking into an enormous oven with the heat full on. The trees hung limp and motionless, while the comet burnt so brightly that you couldn't look at it. Moomintroll ran across the sand and into the wood, shouting at the top of his voice: 'Ahoy! Silk-monkey! Where are you? Silk-monkey!'

In the red gloom under the trees not a breath of life stirred: all the small creatures had hidden themselves underground and were cowering there, silent and afraid. Only Moomintroll ran through the wood. He stopped and called, then listened and ran on again. At last he stood still and looked at the watch. He only had twelve minutes left: he would have to go back.

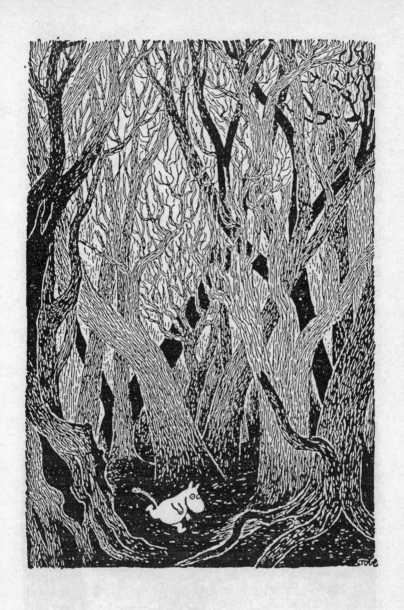

He gave one last yell, and this time to his joy a faint sound came back in reply. He put his paws to his mouth and called again, and the answer came nearer. A moment later the silk-monkey swung down from a tree in front of him. 'Well, well,' she chattered, 'fancy meeting you. I was just wondering . . .'

'We haven't time to talk now,' interrupted Moomintroll. 'Just follow me to the cave as quickly as you can, otherwise something terrible will happen to us.'

They set off as fast as they could, the silk-monkey laughing and screaming and asking questions without the faintest notion of what was happening. 'Is it something exciting?' she babbled, throwing herself from branch to branch in great glee. She thought it was all very amusing – some kind of race perhaps.

Moomintroll had never run so fast in his life. Now and then he looked at the watch and that seemed to be going faster than usual as well. Only four minutes left!

They came out on to the beach . . . three minutes! Oh

how difficult it was to run on the sand. Moomintroll clutched the silk-monkey's paw and together they made a last headlong dash.

Moominmamma was waiting outside the cave, and when she caught sight of them she started waving her arms and shouting: 'Quickly children! Run! Run!'

They scrambled wildly up the rock, and Moominmamma caught hold of them and pushed them through the opening in front of her.

'Oh, thank goodness!' gasped the Snork maiden, and she slowly began to get her normal colour back, because she had been pink with worry for the last twenty minutes. 'You got back in time – my own Moomintroll!'

Then they all heard a dreadful sound outside – a great hissing roar.

All of them except the Hemulen, who was occupied with his stamps, and the Muskrat who was stuck in the basin of hot water, threw themselves flat on the floor in a heap. The lamp went out and they were in complete darkness.

The comet was diving headlong to earth. It was exactly forty-two minutes and four seconds past eight. There was a rush of air as if a million rockets were being let off at once, and the earth shook. The Hemulen fell on his face among the stamps, Sniff yelled at the top of his voice, and Snufkin pulled his hat even farther down over his nose for protection.

The comet roared with its flaming tail right through the valley, across the forest and the mountains, and then disappeared again over the edge of the world.

If it had come a tiny bit nearer to the earth I am quite sure that none of us would be here now. But it just gave a whisk of its tail and swept off to another solar system far away, and it has never been seen since.

But in the cave they didn't know all this. They thought everything had been burnt up or smashed to atoms when the comet came down, and that their cave was the only thing left in the whole world. They listened and listened, but all they heard was silence.

'Mamma,' said Moomintroll, 'is it all over now?'

'Yes, it's over, my little Moomin-child,' said his mother. 'Now everything is all right, and you must go to sleep. You must all go to sleep, my dears. Don't cry Sniff, there's no danger now.'

The Snork maiden was trembling. 'Wasn't it dreadful?' she said.

'Don't think about it any more,' said Moominmamma. 'Cuddle up to me, little silk-monkey, and keep warm. I'm going to sing you all a lullaby.' And this is what she sang:

> Snuggle up close, and shut your eyes tight,
> And sleep without dreaming the whole of the night.
> The comet is gone, and your mother is near
> To keep you from harm till the morning is here.

And presently they dropped off to sleep, one by one, until at last it was quite quiet and peaceful in the cave.

CHAPTER 12

Which is about the end of the story.

MOOMINTROLL was the first to wake up next morning. For a long time he couldn't remember where he was, and when it all came back to him he got up at once, tiptoed cautiously to the mouth of the cave, gingerly lifted the blanket and looked out.

What a sight met his eyes! The sky was no longer red, but a beautiful blue once again, and the morning sun shone in its usual place, looking as though it had been freshly polished. Moomintroll sat down and turned his face up to it, shutting his eyes and heaving a deep sigh of happiness.

After a time the Snork maiden came creeping out of the cave and sat down beside him.

'Well, the sky, the sun and the rocks are still here anyway,' she said solemnly.

'And look! The sea is coming back,' whispered Moomintroll. And there it was rolling tirelessly in towards them, glittering and gleaming like soft blue silk, the same old sea that they had always loved!

All the little sea creatures came out of the mud where they had taken refuge and darted happily up to the surface; the seaweed and water plants slowly began to grow towards the sun, and out to sea a flock of sea-gulls appeared and were soon circling over the beach.

In the cave they were waking up one by one and blinking with surprise. The night seemed to them like a terrible black and red dream, and the Hemulen was really the only one who wasn't amazed at the sunshine and blue sea. He just carried his stamps down on to the sand and said: 'Now I'm going to put my watermarks in order for the seventh time, and woe-betide anyone who disturbs me – be he of the Moomin, Snork or Snufkin tribe.'

The Muskrat snorted, gave his whiskers a brushing, and wandered off to see if his hammock was still about.

'Now I've got a new chapter for my memoirs,' said Moominpappa. 'My goodness! That book is going to be exciting when it's finished.'

'It certainly is, dear,' said Moominmamma. 'But so many exciting things happen to us that I'm afraid the book will never get finished. Oh, what a joy it is to see the sun again!'

Sniff danced with his tail in a bow and held his dagger up to the sun so that the opals shone. Then he set off with the silk-monkey to see if there were any crabs left after the catastrophe.

Meanwhile Snufkin had taken out his mouth-organ and was giving it another try. All the notes had come back, even the little ones, so that he could play to his heart's content.

Moomintroll went into the cave, dug up his pearls and lay them in the Snork maiden's lap.

'These are for you,' he said, 'so that you can decorate yourself all over the place, and be the most beautiful Snork maiden in the world.'

But the biggest pearl of all he gave to his mother to wear in her nose.

'Oh Moomintroll! How beautiful!' she said. 'But now I want to know what has happened. Do you think the wood is still there, and the house, and the kitchen-garden?'

'I think everything is still there,' said Moomintroll. 'Come with me and have a look.'